no ordinary Love Song

First published 2011 by Walker Books Ltd
87 Vauxhall Walk, London SE11 5HJ

2 4 6 8 10 9 7 5 3 1

Text © 2011 Alison Prince
Cover photograph © photolibrary. All rights reserved
Cover photograph © Don Farrall/Getty Images

This book has been typeset in Fairfield

Printed and bound in Great Britain by Clays Ltd, St Ives plc

British Library Cataloguing in Publication Data:
a catalogue record for this book is available from the British Library

ISBN 978-1-4063-0663-7

www.walker.co.uk

no ordinary Love Song

Alison Prince

**WALKER
BOOKS**

Part 1

Chapter 1

This is such a stupid boat. *Observation Lounge*, it says, but if you sit down you can't see out because the windows are too high. Not that it matters. I don't have to observe what's going past, I've seen it often enough. Islands, sea, sky. Lighthouse on the port side as we slide out of the harbour.

It's stuffy in here. Too many people. Tourists crossing to the island with their kids and dogs and food and buggies and maps. And islanders coming back from Glasgow with carrier bags full of stuff from shoe shops and Marks & Spencer. Boring.

I wanted to bring my laptop but Elaine said I might leave it on the train. Just because I lost my mobile last year. It's not just me, people lose stuff all the time. I saw a thing on TV, all these mobiles in a lost property office, hundreds of them. And bags and coats and radios and guitars. Who'd be stupid enough to forget a guitar? There was even an elephant's foot. And a whole boxful of false teeth, all grinning up from on top of each other, pink and white and the odd bit of gold. Why would people leave their dentures on a train? Perhaps they're really uncomfortable to wear, like you see women pushing their shoes off after a day's shopping and saying, "My feet are killing me."

There's an Australian family just across from where I'm sitting. They're talking in those wowy voices Aussies have. A woman with brown hair in a ponytail and a man in those long shorts that have a lot of pockets. His hair's shaved so close to his head, he looks bald. The kids run across to the window – a boy of about eight and a younger one who can't see out because he's not tall enough. He's screaming and thumping his brother. An older girl goes over and picks him up.

"There," she says. "That better?" And he stares out, then puts his thumb in his mouth and nods.

She's wearing raggy-edged shorts that are hacked-off jeans. Fantastic legs. Lean and strong, very brown. I don't think she's the kids' big sister, they're both fair like the shaven-headed man and she's kind of coffee colour, like the Malaysian people I saw in Kuala Lumpur. Maybe she's an au pair. Don't know that she's old enough, she looks about sixteen, same as me. She shifts the little boy to sit astride her hip, and points.

"See that bit of land over there, where the water meets the sky?"

He nods.

"That's where Gran lives," she tells him. "And we're going to live there, too."

She's wearing chunky sandals. Could be made of car tyres, like the ones in Elaine's *Save the Earth* catalogues.

Elaine tries to be nice. I mean, she's my mother and everything, but she's so stupid. How can she really think things can get better? Can't she see we've gone too far? There are too many humans, we've mucked it all up. But it must be tough for her to admit that having Jess and me added two more people and made things that bit worse.

Fathers are different. At least, mine is. McCasky doesn't care, he just gets on with running the firm and making money. Or not. He keeps moaning about the financial situation. He's got a heap of sexy calendars from some Italian tyre company called Pirelli in his desk drawer. They're ancient but he says they're an investment. Who's he kidding, he just likes photos of girls.

Pirelli. How crazy was that, getting the first boat this morning to go to the mainland and see a shrink called Pirelli. He didn't even sound Italian. Rimless glasses, yellow polo shirt. Waste of time. Just because the school thinks I'm a nutter. It isn't nuts to pack in their stupid work and tell them there's no point. Schools don't go in for truth, they just apply the system. And I'm not in their system. I'd rather be dead. Well, sometimes. It's better when I'm playing music. That's all that matters, really.

The little kid starts kicking his feet to get down. "Want a drink," he says.

"OK," says the girl. "Let's ask Mum."

She turns round with the kid on her hip, and meets my eye. Most people look away if I catch them staring because my hair embarrasses them. OK, it's meant to. It's halfway down my back and bright orange, and combing it is not an option. I had a long session in the bathroom with a packet of stuff called Caribbean Dawn after Liam in our band started calling me Blondie. It turned out absolutely fluorescent, like highlights but all over. When McCasky saw it, his eyes bulged and I thought he was going to have a heart attack. But he didn't, unfortunately. He just said, "Jesus Christ," and went to watch the telly with a whisky.

The girl seems to think orange is fine, she's giving me a big smile. Her own hair is black and curly like a dog's fur and – this is weird – I want to run my fingers through it. I want to feel the warm hardness of her head under my hand.

Mustn't stare. My face is going red, and I've got this colossally sexy feeling. It shouldn't happen when other people are around. It's private. It belongs with dreams and bed. I get up and blunder out of the lounge, hardly seeing where I'm going. Push open the door that leads out to the deck, step over the splash-ledge, lean on the rail.

I'm staring down at the white bow wave that keeps curling over itself beside the ferry, but even that seems sexy. The wind of the ship's movement blows my hair all over the place, but it cools my hot face a bit. Must think of something dull, calm down.

Think about painting all these railings white every year to keep them from rusting. Think about the car deck. Lorries, vans, cars, mobile homes lumbering around the lanes so nobody can pass. Tourists. We couldn't do without them but some of them are such idiots. That girl, though.

Why didn't I smile back when she smiled at me? Perhaps I did. Can't have done it right or I might be talking to her by now. Don't know what I'd say. Ask if she's coming to the island. Stupid, of course she is, or she wouldn't be on the boat. I could have asked her what her name is. She'd have told me, then I'd have said, *I'm Callum McCasky, Cal for short.* Then what?

Dunno. I don't do talking much, only to Jess and she's my sister so it doesn't count.

Yeah, could have been a conversation opportunity and I missed it. What an idiot.

I go on looking at the sea while gulls drift around in case a tourist starts lobbing sandwich crusts.

Maybe I could have another try.

Haul the door open, go back into the non-observation lounge.

The Aussie family isn't there. Gone to the cafeteria, probably. I sit down and try to go on thinking about dull stuff. Lost property. False teeth. When the guy came to talk about careers I said I might do dentistry, because he'd mentioned it in his list of very good jobs.

Boring.

Not boring enough.

I want to look at the girl again.

Chopping onions, Elaine's eyes stung. *Shouldn't have bought this white kind*, she thought, *they're always killers.* The brown-skinned ones in the garden would be milder, but they weren't ready yet. She rubbed her eyes with the back of her wrist and scooped the onions into the hot oil in the iron pot, then started peeling garlic. Barnaby, the tabby cat, sneezed for about the fourth time as he sat hopefully at her feet, and scrubbed at his nose with almost the same movement as her own.

"I know," she said to him. "You hate onions. But if you want a bit of meat you'll just have to put up with it."

She was not in the best of tempers. It had been a tough day, with five clients, including that skinny woman who kept putting herself on new diets. And she'd been wondering all the time how Callum was getting on in Glasgow. She took the stewing steak out of the fridge and began to cut it up. She didn't much like handling meat, but Fergus was contemptuous of "rabbit food", and he probably needed animal protein, being out in all weathers. She dropped a sinewy bit into the cat-dish on the floor, and Barnaby set about chewing it.

Therapy ought to include the family, she thought again. She'd written to the Education Department and asked if she could be present at Callum's sessions, but got a firm refusal. She still regretted the wasted opportunity. It had come as a relief that the school had at last stopped trying to make Callum shape up, but being excluded from the official approach was very hurtful. *I am part of the problem*, she thought. But talking to Callum about it was impossible. Going to Glasgow together could have been good – there was so seldom a real reason to spend a substantial amount of time alone with her son. She'd have taken the car over. The drive would have been the ideal setting for a conversation. Being side by side was less confrontational than facing each other.

She tipped the meat into the sizzling pot and stirred it with a wooden spoon, then gave Barnaby the rest of the scraps.

"What have you done with Jingle?" she asked him, without serious concern. Ginger Jingle had arrived from the rescue home with a collar and bell – hence his name. Bell or no bell, his distressed previous owners could not prevent his hunting habits. That's why he fetched up in the cat home. Elaine didn't try to stop him hunting. She took his collar off and cleared up leftover bits of mice and rats from the kitchen floor most mornings. Jingle spent a lot of his daylight hours asleep somewhere, naturally enough. But Barnaby was always around for a cuddle.

Automatically, she glanced at the kitchen clock, aware that the ferry would dock in fifty minutes, then gave her head a small shake. *Don't go and meet him*, she told herself. *He can get the bus.* Only yesterday, Fergus had said, "For God's sake, Elaine, stop molly-coddling the boy. He's sixteen. Time he stopped wallying around and got his hands dirty."

Speaking of dirty hands, she'd better go and pull up some carrots. She put the lid on the casserole, turned the heat down and went out to the garden, climbing the steps to the vegetable beds. She paused to nip off a handful of lemon basil, still feeling fretful. It seemed so natural to want to go and meet her son.

Elaine's out there in her garden, I can see her from the window, digging and weeding. I snuck in here and up to my room when I got off the bus, but I want to go up the hill, and she's between me and the gate at the top of the garden. My guitar's lying on the bed but if I start playing she'll know I'm back and we'll have one of those oh-so-caring conversations, "Darling, how did you get on?" I didn't get on. Pirelli was a waste of space. He didn't ask any questions, just rambled on about life on an island, like some tourist who was thinking of coming here. He left these long gaps so I had to tell him something. I hate tourists.

Stand behind the curtain, watch. She glances at her watch, jams the fork in the earth, turns to come down the steps. She's gone in through the kitchen door. I go down the stairs, quietly, and sneak through the conservatory – oh, shit, she's seen me.

"Darling, there you are," she says, knife in hand like a well-meaning Lady Macbeth. "How did you get *on*?"

"OK."

"Was he nice?"

"Yeah, s'pose so."

"Oh, well, that's good." She looks at me with concern. "Are you going out?"

"Just up the hill."

"We'll be eating in an hour."

"I'll be back."

Escape. Up the steps, past the walnut tree.

She's left a wilting pile of weeds on the path. There's your typical human. Kill anything you don't like, make sure you're top of the heap. So stupid, when's it all going to stop. Don't they *know* the Arctic's melting like someone left the central heating on? And it's all our fault, we don't think of anything except our own horrible progress.

I'm running up the path, really pushing the pace. A bit lunatic because the sun's still quite high in the sky, but I like the sweat and the getting out of breath. After about twenty minutes I come to the flat bit where the Forestry have put a wooden bench. I wouldn't stop if there was anyone there, but it's empty, so I sit down and lean forward with my elbows on my knees, panting a bit but not much.

The sea sparkles down there between the trees, looking like it's so harmless.

Ants are scurrying about on the patch of concrete that the bench is set into. They're so busy, they don't take much notice of these lumps that are my feet. I'm so far above their world, I could be God. And that starts a memory replaying. It's not one I want, but it's one of the ones that are hard to get rid of.

In the plane back from Kuala Lumpur, when Elaine and I had been to see her sister Caro, the flight crew started making people lower the blinds although it was still light. But I wanted to see out so I went and stood by a window near the tail of the plane, looking down at this spread of dry, pinkish mountains that went all the way to the mistiness where the horizon was. Fold on fold of bare, empty peaks. The dryness of it made me think I might be getting dehydrated, so I went to the galley to ask for some water. A flight attendant was sitting by the work surface in the dark, with her head on her arms. She got up and handed me a plastic bottle without really opening her eyes.

It would have been different if Jess had come, we'd have been cracking jokes and playing games on the seat-back screen. But she'd gone on a cybernetics course. I know why now. At the time, I still thought she'd be doing music.

I stood there, looking down and drinking the water. The white line of a river was running between the hills, with patches of green because it was making the ground moist enough to grow things. And then there was a town. Tiny lumps of reddish-grey buildings spreading over the landscape like a rash. That's when it hit me. I thought, *Humans are a sickness. We're an eczema on the face of the earth.* I had the empty plastic water bottle in my hand, and the light feel of it was suddenly horrible. The patterned blue carpet under my feet was horrible, too. I couldn't find anything to look at that didn't hurt.

I ended up staring at the ice-crystals on the outside of the window. I don't know why it's freezing when you're a mile closer to the blazing sun, but it is. The little ice structures were kind of comforting, so tiny and perfect. They'd melt when we got near the earth and change back into water vapour, but if the vapour found another aircraft up there in the cold, it would turn into crystals again. So harmless. Not like us.

One of the ants is running across my foot. It stops and waves its feelers. Maybe it's shouting something down to the others. Do ants talk? They might. We never thought whales could talk, but they do. Or sing, or whatever. Elaine has this CD called *Whale Music* that she plays to her aromatherapy victims. Some of them go for Buddhist chant or Vivaldi, but it's surprising how many like the whales. I listen outside the door of her treatment room sometimes.

The ant has run down the slope of my trainer to join the others. It's touching antennae with the first one it meets. They're talking. They really are talking.

Shit, people are coming up the hill. A man in flowered shorts and desert boots. His legs are bright pink. There's a wispy-haired woman panting behind him.

"Mind if we join you?" he says. He sounds American.

The pair of them smell of anti-perspirant or something. A chemical stink. I get up and move away.

"Don't let us disturb you," says the man. He and the woman are staring at my hair like tourists in Africa who've found a primitive person with a bone through his nose. They don't notice they're treading on the ants. They dump their horrible little rucksacks and sit down on the bench. I look at the sun and think I'd better head home. No point in upsetting Elaine.

I wonder if ants mourn their dead.

I'm sprawled on my bed with my laptop, looking up ants.

We got through the meal all right. They gave up asking about Pirelli after a bit. McCasky was going on about the price of timber to local contractors like him. He gets furious that people take their own vans across to the mainland and stock up from B&Q or else buy the stuff online. Elaine made sympathetic noises, the way she always does. Then she turned to me and asked, "Have you got homework, darling?"

She sounded so sympathetic, she might have been asking if I had head lice or TB.

I said, "Yeah. Bit."

I didn't tell her there was piles of it. They keep setting the stuff, but I'm not going to do it. I'm not into work and exams – their whole stupid success game. Count me out.

She said, "If I can give you a hand—"

McCasky said, "Pete's sake, what's the point of homework if he doesn't do it himself?" Elaine smoothed a strand of greying hair behind her ear and looked away. I think she should dye it. Not orange like me, that would be ridiculous, but just blonde or something. But anyway, I said I'd get on with it and came up here to my room. Can't play my guitar or McCasky will know I'm not working. Elaine knows, but she shuts up about it.

The internet is full of stuff about ants. Half the scientists in the world seem to be totally obsessed with them. Weird. Here's a photo of dead ants standing on little boards, skewered by fine pins through their middles like they'd been stuffed. Elaine took me and Jess to some awful natural history museum when we were small and I bawled the place down because of the stuffed animals with their glass eyes. She had to take us to the cafeteria for ice cream to take my mind off it. An early triumph.

Ants are too small to stuff. They must have been pickled in alcohol or something. Like McCasky, except he only takes it internally. Immersion in whisky would be seriously expensive, and the earth-shifting trade is going through a bad time.

Click again. Ants in a long procession, each one carrying pieces of leaf about five times bigger than itself. My father would be dead chuffed if he could get work like that out of his employees. Not a hope. The women in the office are always grumbling about pay and the hours they work. They don't bother to shut up when I'm around.

Must stop thinking about McCasky. Can't help it when he's in the same room because he's large and difficult to ignore, but it's stupid to get stuck with him when he isn't.

Hang on – what was that? Something about singing. Scroll back.

Jeez.

The blue butterfly grub sings quietly... It makes the same sound as the ants' grubs, so they think it is one of their own.

So ants understand music. They get the way it makes you feel, same as we do. How weird is that? I must find out more.

Chapter 2

Elaine stooped over the row of spinach, pulling out the weeds she hadn't had time to deal with yesterday. A small stone had got into her open-toed sandal and she tapped her foot against her other ankle to shake it out. She'd make sure to wash her feet before Fergus came in. He hated her looking like a "peasant".

She missed Jessica. The household seemed lopsided and unbalanced without her daughter's practicality. But Jess had left school straight after the exams and got herself a job in Glasgow with her friend Mairi, whose parents put her up. Sensible, of course, to get some money together before she started uni. She had chosen to study electronics and cybernetics. Jessica was always sensible. She planned to go and see Caro in Kuala Lumpur first, because Caro worked in 3D design in the car industry and that could be useful. Callum had been devastated when she said she wasn't going to do music. She was the lead saxophone in their band called *Sign On*. He said it wouldn't work without her. Could be he was right, because they hadn't met since.

Funny how babies don't change, Elaine thought, remembering when her newborn daughter had been put into her arms. The small face had been very composed, eyes shut, neat little mouth closed. She looked so responsible that Elaine had felt almost embarrassed, as if the baby had been sent as the organizer she had always needed. Callum had been the opposite. When he was born he cried and cried, as if he'd wanted to stay safe inside her instead of being pushed out to begin the business of having a life. He still didn't seem to like it much.

A nettle among the weeds stung her fingers and thumb, and she groped deeper to where its yellow roots had no defence and pulled it out. Callum wasn't a little boy any more. These days, when he bothered to communicate at all, he made her feel old and silly. Fifty-one wasn't old, but there was no way she could tell him she still felt young inside, same as she always had been. He'd laugh, or walk away. More likely walk away – he didn't do much laughing these days. It was very worrying.

Morning break. The others are outside, eating crisps and tearing the wrappers off chocolate bars. I'm getting talked at by Mrs Mack. We're standing beside the whiteboard after she called me back from going out with the others.

People call her the Goth, because she's been dyeing her hair dead black ever since it started going grey. I don't understand this thing about hair colour. Blonde is normal, blue rinse for oldies is OK, black is wacky. Orange is totally unmentionable.

"I know you're having a lot of difficulties, but – look, sit down."

We sit on chairs on either side of one of the tables. The sun's coming in through the windows. My orange hair curtain is very bright. Being behind it is good.

Seems she's just clocked that I'm not doing homework. Not for her, and not for the other teachers either. They must have been getting together.

"When I spoke to your mum and dad at Parents' Evening they said you'd be aiming at a university place. You're certainly well able to do so."

She pauses. I don't say anything, so she ploughs on.

"If you don't intend to study, I feel we should be helping you to find a job. The last thing you want is to be drifting around with nothing to do. Your father takes on trainees, doesn't he – maybe he could help you."

She can forget that, right away, it's a seriously bum idea. Push the hair back, look anguished. Counter-attack.

"You're saying I've got to leave?"

"I wouldn't go that far," she says.

She's the Pupil Support Adviser, so she won't want a reputation for chucking people out.

She back-pedals a bit. "I know you've been doing these therapy sessions, and I do hope they've been helpful. But there's no point in sitting in lessons and learning nothing, is there?"

Wrong. I can think about all sorts of other stuff while I'm not listening to lessons, I'm really good at that. Music, mostly. Tunes. Harmonic progressions. Miss Irvine says I ought to do music as a career. I only put down dentistry because it sounded respectable. It was before I stopped caring, anyway. Before seeing humans as eczema. Before the polar bear standing on that one bit of ice in the sea. Before the dolphins…

The Goth is waiting for me to say something. I re-run what she said. Oh, yeah. No point.

What does she mean, *point*? She and her sort don't have a point. They're not into finding things out, they just do remembering and test-passing. Well, sod that. If I want to learn anything, I use the internet.

Maybe she's right and I ought to leave. It's easier to stay here, though. I don't have to decide anything. But she's droning on.

"Sooner or later, we all have to find some commitment…"

Yeah, yeah, heard it all before. I let the words go on like a conveyor belt, and switch off the attention button. Pink Floyd had it right about the wall. Just another brick. The Goth's trying to lick me into brick shape.

The words have stopped. She's looking a bit bothered.

She was the one who fixed the sessions with Pirelli in the first place, so she's well out of order.

"All right," she says. "Don't worry about it too much. I can see you're feeling a bit depressed."

Depressed isn't the word for it. What do you do when you're stuck with being a human? Part of the big disease that's going to kill everything? Yippee, buy another Mars bar?

"If I can help in any way, just let me know," she goes on. "But meanwhile, you might find that doing some work is actually quite helpful."

"Yeah," I say, trying to look as if I'm thinking about it. "Thanks."

And the bell goes.

I might print some of the ant pictures off and put them on my wall, really big. Ants floor to ceiling.

That's the McCaskymobile turning into the yard now, I can hear it outside. Engine off, car door slam, key in house door, open, he's coming in. He'll be picking up the letter that was on the mat when I came in from school. I turned it over and saw it was from the Education Department so I left it where it was and came up here.

Size for size, ants are a lot more intelligent than humans.

I'm trying to concentrate on the screen, but my mind is jumping about.

"Elaine?" he shouts.

There's a faint squeak from somewhere. Could be she's in the bath.

A lavender candle burned gently beside the tiled wall. Elaine had looked forward to this for the past hour. *I need to wallow*, she thought. *Like a hippopotamus.* The water was pleasantly hot, laced with tea tree to ward off any bacteria from the woman whose bulky body she had been working on. Her hands ached from trying to feel through the thick layer of fat to ease the muscles of the solid back and shoulders.

Fergus couldn't understand why she kept on doing therapy. Only last night, he'd said, "Money-wise, it's not worth your while. You could use your time better."

He didn't understand *giving*, she thought. She rested her head on the waterproof cushion she'd hung over the edge of the bath and closed her eyes, feeling the hot water rising into her hair. You had to give, otherwise there was no room for new ideas and understandings to come in.

"Elaine! You up there?"

He sounded irritable, but not furious. Couldn't be an emergency, then.

She heaved herself up and the water sloshed off her wet hippopotamus shoulders.

"Coming!" she called, and reached for a towel.

* * *

Hell. He's coming up. I can hear his footsteps on the stairs.

He opens the door without knocking and walks in. He's standing behind me, looking at the ants on the computer.

"Interesting?" he says.

"Biology." Well, it's true.

"Spare a minute?"

No choice. I swivel round.

He shows me the letter. "You know about this?"

"What?"

He hands it to me.

Dear Mr and Mrs McCasky,

We are aware of course that Callum is now attending sessions with Dr Pirelli at the Educational Psychology Unit, and we hope this will help with his problems. However, as you probably know, he has ceased to do any homework, and a recent interview with our Pupil Support teacher suggests that he has no interest in any further education. We welcome his willingness to attend the Psychology Unit sessions, but the further outlook continues to present problems.

We feel we should discuss the situation with you and come to a decision about whether continuation at school would be in Callum's best interests. Perhaps you would be good enough to telephone my secretary for an appointment.

                              *   *   *

Shit-hit-the-fan time.

"So what's all this about?" McCasky asks.

"Don't know."

He shuts his eyes for a moment. I can hear him thinking, *God give me patience*. He takes a breath and says,
"Why aren't you doing your homework?"

I shrug. No point in trying to explain. We'd be into a row
straight away, and he never understands anyway so why try.

"Is it too hard?" he says.

"No."

"Too much of it? More than you can fit in?"

"No."

He's gone red. Why does this always happen?

"If you understand the bloody stuff," he says, "why the
fuck don't you just get on and do it?"

Elaine has come to the doorway behind him, in a white
towelling bathrobe.

"There's some tea downstairs," she says, like she's trying to coax a wayward horse. McCasky utters a kind of bel-
low and barges past her and down the stairs.

She looks at me but I turn back to the screen. She's
going to say something very patient that I can't argue with.

"Come down when you're ready, love."

Aaargh. I knew it.

I keep looking at the ants, and she leaves the room. She
even shuts the door. Very quietly.

* * *

Glasgow Central. I tried to phone Jess from home, but her mobile was off. I texted her on the boat to say I was coming over to see the rubber-tyres man and she said *c u glas cent if poss*. But she wasn't here when I came off the train this morning. This is her day off from HMV but most likely she and Mairi are flat-hunting. McCasky says buying a flat makes more sense than renting, because I can live in it later if I get my act together and go to uni. Mairi will pay him rent for the time she's sharing it with Jess. All neatly planned.

I'm hanging about beside the big timetables that stick out on boards, where Jess will see me if she comes. The station is full of noise and people walking about. School kids in superior uniforms that cost a bomb, the kind whose parents send them on a train journey to a posh school. The others walk or bus to whatever educational crap centre is nearest.

The floor of this station is a pale cream colour, very smooth. Marble or something. There's a guy wooshing around on a sweeper machine, clearing up the crisps bags and stuff. They took the bins away in case some terrorist stuck a bomb in one.

Pirelli asked what I'd tell a new kid who came to live on the island.

I said, "Tell him about what?"

He said, "Anything, really. School, that sort of thing."

What *you* think about school, he meant. Nice try.

I said, "Up to him, isn't it?"

"How do you mean?"

"If he likes it, fine."

"And if not?"

"Then he's got to put up with it."

Pirelli didn't ask if I was putting up with it, just asked what else I liked. So I said music. He went on looking hopeful so I told him about the band. He asked what it was called. I said *Sign On* but it was more like *Sign Off* now. He thought that was quite funny but he asked why, so I told him about Jess leaving. He said maybe someone would crop up to replace her.

He didn't write anything down, just sat there while I did the talking. What a waste of time. Anyone could do that. Wonder what he gets paid.

"Hi," says Jess.

"Oh, hi."

Mairi is with her. Fair-haired, skinny. Useless at music. I don't know what Jess sees in her.

"So how was the inflatable man today?" Jess asks. "Got you bouncing back?"

"Nah," I say, "I got tyred."

We've always done this words thing.

"Punctured his ego?"

"Bit of a let-down."

"But you're not flat yet."

"You two, what are you like?" says Mairi.

I miss the laughs now Jess isn't at home.

"Sorry we're so late," she says. "We were in Maryhill and the bus took ages."

The big clock under the glass roof says we've got seven minutes.

"No problem," I say.

But I don't know what to say in seven minutes, 'specially with Mairi hanging around. Six minutes now, the hand's moved on. Only four, really, allowing time to get the train. This station's very big.

"Did you find a flat?" I ask.

"Not for definite."

"The Maryhill one was shite," says Mairi.

Jess says, "There's one in Partick that's great, but it's too expensive."

I don't know the places they're talking about. Cities are rubbish, anyway. Too many people.

I wish Jess was coming home, but she'll be going back with Mairi to her parents' house in Cumbernauld. She says it's quite a long bus ride from Glasgow, but at least it's on the mainland.

She knows what I'm thinking.

"We're working tomorrow, and we start at eight-thirty," she says.

"Sure," I say.

There's no point in dragging this out.

"Look, I'll have to go."

"Sure. Phone me, right?"

"Yeah."

I nearly add, *if your mobile's on*. But there's no point in that, either. We thump loosely clenched fists, the way we always have, and I turn and walk off.

The Aussie family aren't on the boat of course. Why would they be? It was just one chance, and I blew it. The place where she stood by the window with the little kid on her hip is empty.

Chapter 3

Register time, Monday morning. The Goth comes in with – I can't believe it.

I duck my head so my hair falls across my face.

It's her. In school uniform, not the raggy shorts. But the same brown skin. The same short, curly black hair.

She's bound to recognize me. Nobody else here has got orange hair halfway down their back. I can't look up, but the room is full of the fact that she's here. It's like you can't look at the sun though it's all round you.

"We have a newcomer to the school," the Goth says. "Kerry Donovan. She and her family have come all the way from Australia. I'm sure you will make Kerry welcome and help her to find her way around the building. I know it's only a couple of weeks before the summer break, but her parents thought it would be nice for her to meet people before we start the new term. Would someone like to be Kerry's buddy, so she has a friend who will help her if there's anything she doesn't know about?"

Half a dozen hands go up, all girls of course.

"Megan, then. Thank you very much. Nobody need feel left out, you can all be helpful. There's nothing like having lots of friends, is there?"

Kerry Donovan. It's a name with a good sound.

She goes to sit down beside Megan. Most of the girls are smiling at her. The boys start talking again among themselves. A couple of them glance across at Kerry then look away in case anyone thinks they're interested. I don't want them looking at her. I don't want to share anything about her, she's private, they're not to even think about her. But she'll never know.

The bell goes.

Maths.

Kerry.

I like thinking of her name. It's break time and Megan and her mates are fussing round her like tugs guiding a big ship. I keep imagining I could go up and say, "Hi, I saw you on the boat." But I can't. They'd giggle and nudge each other. She might giggle, too. And the boys would ask afterwards, "You keen on her or something?"

It's not like that. Not like they mean, anyway. She's a kind of dream.

The sun is hot again. The girls have settled on a bench with Kerry. I go and perch on one of the bollards by the car park, eating a packet of crisps. Nobody will know if I'm looking at her, because my hair is over my face. And it's not their business anyway.

The man standing on the doorstep looked slightly battered, Elaine thought. He wore a crumpled linen jacket and his face was deeply pitted as if from severe teenage acne.

"Andrew Duncan," he said.

"Do come in." He was dead on time for his appointment.

He wiped his feet carefully although it was a perfectly dry day. "I think you know my sister," he said. "Patsy Carradine. I'm staying with her for a bit. She persuaded me to come."

Elaine knew that. Patsy was a frequent client, regarding massage as a way to keep her formidable fitness topped up. "The treatment room's upstairs," she said. "I hope you don't mind."

Most of her patients were women, and they were happy to follow her up the rather narrow stairs, chatting about what they'd been doing or admiring the pictures on the walls. With men, she always had a slight concern that they might laugh with their mates afterwards about how they'd wondered if they were being taken to a bedroom. The man behind her didn't seem likely to raise a mental eyebrow, though. Too polite. Or maybe too bored. He'd been talked into this, after all. It wasn't his idea.

"Here we are," she said. The pale lavender walls were comforting, she always thought, and the view across the bay to the open sea was a reliable pleasure. "Do sit down. Is it all right if I call you Andrew?"

"Yes."

"Would you like a glass of water?"

"No, thanks."

He wasn't going to be easy, she thought. Not offering any information.

She ran through the preliminary explanation about how important it was to look at all aspects, as this therapy treated the whole person, and he nodded.

She had been trained never to write things down as she questioned a patient. It destroyed their confidence and made the clinical relationship too distant. But it did involve some careful remembering.

She knew a bit already from what Patsy had said. He lived in Kilmarnock, on the mainland. He'd seen their mother through cancer but she died a few weeks ago. And he was thinking of coming to live here. Better check that.

"Patsy says you may be thinking of a move to the island?"

"It's a possibility. Circumstances have changed recently so I'm free to look at new possibilities."

"You're on your own?"

"Yes." After a pause, he added, "I was married but she found someone else."

"Children?"

"Daughter studying molecular biology at Cambridge. Her mother got custody when we split. Vicky was four years old. I've not seen much of her since. I've been out of the country a lot."

"Working?"

"I'm a press photographer. Or was. Specialized in war zones."

"Will you go back to that?"

"Probably not."

Elaine changed tack.

"How's your general health?"

He shrugged. "So-so. I got blown up in Beirut. They flew me home and it was a bit touch and go. I'm OK now. The odd aches and pains. Getting old, I suppose."

"How old?"

"Fifty-two."

She'd have guessed nearer sixty.

"Just a year older than me," she said, with faint reproof.

He gave her the conventionally polite response.

"You look at least a decade younger, if I may say so."

She felt wrong-footed. Her comment had been unprofessional, but he had the good manners of someone used to diplomacy. *More to him than meets the eye, perhaps.* She went back to the routine queries.

"Any history of childhood illness?"

"Eczema." He gestured faintly at his pitted face.

"Scratched myself to bits."

"Does it still bother you?"

"No. Grew out of it, I suppose."

"So how do you generally feel?"

He looked out of the window at the sea, then said, "Patsy thinks I'm depressed."

"What do you think?"

He turned his hands palm up then turned them back.

"I think I'm a useless prat," he said. And smiled to show it was a joke.

"You're not useless," Elaine said firmly. "You're out of touch with your potential, that's all."

She stood up before he could say anything else.

"Now, I'm just going to wash my hands. If you'd like to take everything off down to your underpants and hop onto the couch, I'll be back in a minute." She handed him a big, soft bath sheet. "Put this over you."

Downstairs, she washed her hands as she had said, but took a few minutes to note down his replies, adding, *Needs stimulation and comfort*. Basil, then, and nutmeg, to help with mental fatigue. Geranium, for balance. And a touch of cypress, to give an astringent edge. Men usually liked the smell, they found it reassuring.

He was lying flat on his back when she went back upstairs, totally covered by the towel, which he had arranged neatly, all its edges straight. He'd taken his glasses off and put them in their case on the windowsill, and his eyes were shut. She didn't speak to him and moved quietly as she added her essential oils to almond oil as a carrier then warmed them and mixed them. She turned the towel back from his left foot, cradled it firmly between her hands for a moment, then began to work.

There was a long scar on his right thigh and she thought about the incident in Beirut, wondering what had happened. It was not until nearly an hour later, when she lifted the towel from his upper body, that she saw the puckered emptiness on the side of his chest where ribs had been shattered.

The photo on the screen shows a man holding his arm out over a massive ant hill somewhere in Africa. It's a big grey thing, fatter than a council wheelie bin and tall enough to reach his hand. How do ants manage to make a thing that size?

My phone rings.

"Hi," says Jess. "How're you doing?"

"OK."

She hasn't been in touch since that quick meeting in Glasgow. I tried her when I was there the next time but she didn't answer.

Click on. Dozens of anthills, like a city. Weird.

"Sorry I've been a bit out of touch," she says. "I've got all this reading to do before term starts, so I've been trying to fit some of that in as well as working and flat-hunting."

She's rushing on, the way she always does. "Hey, listen – I know you're not into cybernetics and all that, but I got a book out of the library that's on the list, and it's really interesting. You know how a human brain looks like just a single thing, just a white lump?"

"Yeah. Cold porridge."

"Right. But it works as a huge collection of bits, same as computers do. New bits keep coming all the time while others go."

"That right?"

I'm not really listening. I click on to the next page, but it's solid text by some scientist. Try the next one. A picture of a table in some old-fashioned place, with its legs standing in tins of paraffin...

"This book says the brain isn't a super-machine, it's more like a collective community. And if you want to construct the perfect artificial one, that's a huge idea."

There's no way I'd want to construct an artificial brain. She ought to have done music. Better sound interested, though.

"Collective community? Like, Zen monks or something?"

"No, idiot. Like an ant heap."

"A *what*?"

"The ant heap is an exact model of how the brain works. Isn't that amazing?"

I start to laugh, but she's still explaining.

"That's the key to designing intelligent computers. They function exactly like an ant heap does. Excuse me, but why is that so funny?"

She's miffed. Better watch it or she'll hang up.

"Jess, listen – you know what I'm doing right now? I'm on the internet. Looking up ants."

"Go on?" There's a puzzled pause. "Why?"

"I was up the hill, a couple of weekends back. I sat down on that seat, you know the one, looking over the bay."

"And?"

"There were these ants. I was watching them. One of them ran over my foot. Then a couple of tourists came up. I moved off the bench and they came to sit down on it, and they trod all over the ants."

"Probably didn't see them."

"I don't mean they did it on purpose, that's not the point. Thing is, the ants were rushing around and I wondered if they were upset about the ones that had been killed. It seemed like they were talking to each other and I wondered if they could. So when I got back I Googled ants and all this stuff came up."

"F-*ant*-astic!" says Jess, not to start a word game, just out of habit. "I don't think they do talk – at least, not in language like we use. They're kind of – components. Bits. But each bit is alive."

"They can hear things."

Something about blue moth caterpillars singing to

them. Can't remember what the page actually said.

"Yes. And smell things. They use pheromones, they're like scents … hardly aware of. Humans … them, too … got a lot to do with … attracted to each other."

Her phone is breaking up. Sounds like she's running out of battery.

"… ants … upset. Not in the same way … people … each … just a par…"

It'll cut off in a minute.

" …attery," her distant voice says. "… call … orrow…"

There's some more, but I can't hear it.

"OK?" I say, though she's probably gone. "Bye."

Chapter 4

The girls' rugby team is out on the field. I'm watching from the upstairs window near the music department. Most people have gone home but we've been practising for a fundraising concert to send stuff to a school in Malawi and I'm waiting for the late bus. Kerry is out there with the others. She won't see me behind the glass.

I'm not into rugby, I'm too skinny and I don't see the point, but the way the girls play is awesome. The quick ones do the attacking stuff but the heavy girls are in there, too, running to be in the right place, catching, kicking hard. Grab, duck, elbow, push. Kerry's got the ball, she's running with it. One of the other team has grabbed her by the neck, pulling her sideways. They've both crashed down – the ball goes bouncing off in that zigzag way, there's a pile of people falling over the top of Kerry. Jeez, it looks awful. Miss Armitage is running across, blowing her whistle. They're getting up. Kerry's the last to get to her feet. She's furious, shouting at the girl who pulled her over, shaking a fist in her face. Miss Armitage is separating them, telling Kerry to cool it.

The Head thought rugby was too tough for females, so he wouldn't let the girls form a side for ages. But the boys got the girls in to make up a team if they were short, so he had to give in because they were playing anyway.

Miss Armitage looks at her watch and blows a long blast on the whistle. Someone tosses the ball to her and she catches it in that neat way PE people have and tucks it under her arm. They're all walking in to get changed. Kerry is last, walking on her own. She looks very fed up.

The bus is crowded. I'm sitting by the window, two rows behind the driver's seat. He starts the engine, then looks round to see if people are settled. They're not, of course.

"Just sit down," he shouts. "Doesn't matter where."

Kerry's one of the ones still standing up. She's saying something over her shoulder to one of the other girls as she sits herself in the empty seat beside me, so her head's turned away. The bus starts. She heaves her sports bag onto her knees and sees me.

"Oh, hi," she says. Gives me that big smile.

"Hi."

"You were on the boat, weren't you."

"Yeah."

I ought to say something intelligent but I've gone blank.

"Where d'you live?" she asks.

"Kilkeddie."

"Me too. That your house with the concrete yard outside? It's got McCasky Groundworks on a sign."

"Yeah."

I tuck some of my hair behind my ear. Bad about the concrete.

"There's a garden behind the house," I tell her. "It goes up the hill."

"Sounds great," she says.

Her Australian twang sounds like a TV cricket commentary. McCasky is keen on cricket. Watches it on Sunday afternoons.

"I been meaning to go up there, have a look around." Then she laughs. "This liddle island cracks me up. You can drive right round it in a coupla hours. Only I can't drive a car here."

"Did you drive in Australia?"

"I've been driving since I was ten. Not legal – just off-road. We had a big place. Horses and stuff – Mum ran a trekking centre. Plenty of room to drive, it was three miles down to the billabong, and that was still on our patch."

Three *miles*. All that space, completely your own. No tourists in it. Wow.

"Don't you miss it?"

"Well, kinda," she says. "I like the way it's so green here, though. All these liddle rivers everywhere."

"They're called burns."

"I know. My mum was born here. She went travelling and met someone she liked, and married him."

Maybe they'll go back there. Panic. Try to sound calm.

"Are you here to stay?"

"Yeah, we sold everything up. See, Gran's getting a bit doo-lally. If she's alone in the house she starts banging on the windows and shouting at people to save her. She thinks she's in prison, it's really sad. There's a nurse comes in twice a day, but Grandpa has to stay with her the rest of the time. So he can't keep running the business."

"A business on the island?"

"Yeah. Sports shop and bike hire."

"Oh, right." There's only one. "The Outdoor Shop in Colbeag. Kenny Murdo."

"That's it. Dad reckons it's got potential."

I nod and try to look intelligent, but I don't know about things like potential. Don't want to. There's a bit of a silence. I'm staring out of the window in a state of kick-self. Come on, say something. She's sitting right here beside me, how magic is that? But I can't find any words.

"Dad thinks he might do camping gear," she goes on. "And kayaks, maybe. He rented out speedboats back home but we had these big lakes and the water was pretty flat. It's rougher on the sea."

"Yeah."

More silence. This is so stupid.

The bus is going up the hill through the Forestry. She's looking across at the big trees going past on our left. I'm staring out of the window beside me, the other way. Now we're out on the straight bit. I can see over the hedge to the wreckage where they felled all the Sitka two years back. Gorse has grown among the dead stumps. Yellow flowers, masses of dark prickles. Shrubby birch coming up. But it's trenched and ruined, stones and torn-up roots like there's been a war there. I saw a film once about World War I, with army farriers going round shooting injured horses. Animals don't have wars, they just get dragged into human ones. It's so awful, being human. I feel kind of sick all the time.

Kayaks, she was talking about. *Kayaks*. Come on, get it together. *Say* something.

"The Outdoor Education lot have kayaks."

"Go on? You into boats?"

"Not really." Good start, keep going. "I saw you playing rugby. I was up in the music department."

"Did you see that high tackle?" she asks. "What a cow – she had me round the neck, pulled me down. That's totally against the rules. So I gave her a mouthful, like anyone would – and the PE teacher told me off for using bad language. Like it was *my* fault!"

We're coming down the hill into the village.

"They were all on top of you," I say. "I thought you'd be an ambulance case."

"Nah, I was OK. But I thought it was pretty crap, the way I got told off and she didn't."

The bus is coming to a halt.

"Lots of things are crap."

"Could be right," she says.

The door hisses open and she gets up with the others. Looks back and says, "See you tomorrow."

She's crossing the road in front of the bus. Giving me a wave. I do my royal to-and-fro of the hand like the Queen as the bus moves off. She's laughing.

We've finished the lasagne. I'm peeling a banana. McCasky cuts a hunk of cheese. He's looking at me.

"So how's it going in Glasgow?"

"OK."

He arranges a bit of cheese on his bread, bites it off, chews, swallows.

"Just talk, is it?"

"Yeah."

Elaine gets up from the table. "Coffee?" she asks.

McCasky gives her a nod, but he keeps on.

"Is it useful?"

"Don't know, really."

"What do you talk *about*?"

"Music. Going up the hill. Anything, really."

"There's some shortbread," says Elaine. "Or Jaffa Cakes."

"So you go all the way to Glasgow to talk to this guy

about going up the hill and playing music," McCasky says, like he's trying to get it straight in his head.

"Sort of, yes."

He does some more eating while he thinks about that.

"But you can't talk to your mother or me."

The banana in my hand is very pale and clean, with its yellow skin dangling over my fingers. I haven't bitten the top off it yet. Bob Heaney says he can't face a banana after that sex talk last term, but I don't mind. The trick is not to think about it. I don't think about anything much if I can help it. Can't always stop, though.

"You'll get no advice from that banana," McCasky says. "You might as well get on and eat the bloody thing."

But I can't. I just wish I was somewhere else.

"You saw that letter from the school," he goes on. "We've an appointment with the Head next week, to decide if you're staying on or not. Might I ask if you have any views on that?"

"You have to give him space," says Elaine. "He'll talk about it when he's ready."

Why doesn't she keep out of it? Remarks like that are just asking to get trashed.

"Oh, very nice. I'll try that next time someone rings up with water coming through the roof." He puts on a prissy female voice. "*You have to give me space, I'll talk about it when I'm ready.*"

Elaine's face has turned pink, but she's in fighting

mode, like the mouse I rescued from Jingle last week. It bit my finger.

"You know what I mean," she says. "You're grown up. Callum isn't."

He eats the last bit of cheese and pushes his plate away.

"In that case," he says, "perhaps somebody will be good enough to tell me when an enquiry is permitted."

He heaves himself up from the table and walks out. We hear the engine of the pick-up truck start. It sounds very loud in the silence.

Elaine doesn't say anything, but Meaningful Conversation is hanging in the air. Time for a retreat upstairs. I leave the banana on the table. Can't seem to fancy it.

Elaine stacked the plates in the dishwasher. She spooned the left-over vegetables into a bowl, stretched some cling film over them and put them in the fridge, along with Callum's banana, though it would turn grey and have to be dumped eventually. She wiped the table and rinsed the cloth under the tap, then stood with her hands on the edge of the sink. Through the window in front of her, the sun still slanted in, close to the shoulder of the hill. *It's a long time since I've been up there*, she thought. Years. She and Fergus used to walk on the hill a lot with the children when they were small. He used to carry Callum on his shoulders if he got tired. It was different now.

She knew where Fergus had gone – he didn't bother

to keep it secret. Ever since he built the extension to Kitty Reed's house, he'd been back there a ridiculous number of times, on one thin pretext or another. They knew all about it in the office, of course. Gossip stopped quickly if they saw Elaine going past, but with the window open in the hot weather, the latest scraps of scandal and cackles of laughter were easy to hear.

Kitty Reed's extension work had included construction of a swimming pool that gave rise to apparently endless troubles with its pump. Or, Elaine thought sourly, the urgent problem of what to do if a leaf fell in the water. Kitty had brassy hair and a deep suntan (not surprising, with all that lounging by the pool). Her husband spent most of his time in Saudi Arabia.

Elaine put a peppermint tea bag into a mug and waited for the kettle to boil. The galling thing about Kitty Reed was her relaxation and good cheer – exactly the qualities that Elaine tried to help people achieve. She could see very well why Fergus liked her. As a bolt-hole from this house and its complex webs of sensitivity, Kitty's place would be bliss. *I'm not jealous*, she thought in bleak, distinct words, *I just envy him*.

She carried her tea into the garden and sat down at the picnic table Fergus had knocked up after he built the patio. The rumpus at the supper table was still replaying in her mind. What would Callum be thinking, up there in his room? *Maybe I'll phone Jessica*. But she knew what her daughter would say. "Callum's fine, don't worry about him." Jessica never talked about her younger brother. The pair of them had long ago formed a partnership that was proof against all the boring assaults of the adult world. But now that Jess had left school, Callum was on his own. And he wasn't practical like his sister.

What *was* he, then? It had always seemed astonishing to Elaine that she had given birth to this man-child from her female body. She still looked at him with wonder. *Men are so lucky,* she thought. All through their lives, they were free to use their energies as they chose. They did not have to cope with the constant monthly preparation for potential child-birth or with the commitment that closed tight on you like a trap when a baby was born. They didn't understand how that awful surge of love for a child swept all the things you had valued into some insignificant corner, where rust and dust made them unusable when you wanted to retrieve them later. Maybe some did. She mustn't be unfair. But they all seemed to need something else. An absorbing game of some kind. Business or politics, golf or the Chamber of Commerce. Callum didn't seem to have anything, except his music.

He must be very alone, she thought. *I wish I could help him.* But he wouldn't let her.

The last sliver of the sun was slipping away behind the hill, and though the sky was filled with clarity, the warmth was fading. In a minute, she would need to go in for a cardigan.

Chapter 5

Jess has emailed three scanned pages from this old library book about white ants. Termites. The sort that build those big heaps I was looking at. They can eat a whole cow if you leave it tethered so it can't run away. The last page is the really interesting one. It says ant colonies live forever, because they are always renewing themselves.

Jess likes that, of course. We're chatting online. She says:

if brain cd live forever, ud remember back 1000s of years.

I write, *how?*

each cell wd change 1000s times but ud still think u were yourself.

I see what she means. Mr Weir said in Woodwork, "A Chippendale chair is always a Chippendale, even if over the years other craftsmen replace all its legs and its back and its seat." I used to like Mr Weir, but he left. He works as a joiner now, comes to buy stuff from McCasky.

Jess is writing again.

ants been around 100 million yrs

ur kidding!

so a colony remembers 100m yrs back

wow

computer like ant brain, can replace bits. nothing gets 4gotten

She runs on before I can write an answer.

humans r wasteful. cant hand it on when you die, kids start from scratch

cant hand wt on?

all you've found out

like?

wt people mean when they dnt say

computer cant understand that

can if u find way to input

but how does it know who it is?

does it need to?

We were arguing about that for ages. I won in the end, because I said a computer/ant brain would be no good for music, you needed a living body, to play and sing. And dance and feel excited or sad. Jess said you could synthesize the sound, but she didn't have an answer about the dancing and feeling, just said you couldn't be sure.

There will be millions of ants on this hillside. Billions, maybe. Trillions. How many is a trillion? Numbers with a lot of zeros at the end don't mean anything. I know a lot more about ants now. The ones that run around on the surface are just a few, most of them are working away under the earth, looking after young ones, keeping the place clean, carrying food home, exchanging messages.

Come to think of it, the Scottish word for shopping is "messages". My gran never went out without her message bag. Elaine's started using one, too. It's made of some kind of sacking with *Save the Planet* stamped on it in black letters. Too late, of course, but there's no point in telling her. She likes to believe people can be good and save things.

The air's full of midges because it's shady and the burn runs close by the path. My hair keeps most of them off my face and neck, but they get everywhere else, even up my T-shirt, and the bites are dead itchy. Mustn't scratch, or they come up in red lumps. It'll be better further up, when I'm out of the trees.

There are hut circles here, where people used to live about four thousand years ago. They're hidden now because the bracken's so high, but in the winter it's easy to see the stones of the outer wall and the inner one. When I was younger Elaine dragged me along to a local history talk by some old guy who'd written a book about it. He said you always find bracken in places where people used to live because they cooked stuff and dumped the bones and skin. And they shat, so it got fertilized. And he said people took the stones from the hut circles later, to build the sheep-dip and the bothy.

I like the bothy. Most of the roof has fallen in and there's no door, just a sprawling elder tree that you have to duck under. I go in there sometimes and look at the black patch in the middle of the floor where they had the fire. The other end has still got the holes in the wall where bars fitted, to keep the cattle in when the winter got too bad.

At the top of the steep bit where the Forestry has put logs to make steps, I'm out of the trees. Up here, the sky is open and clear. Heather and blueberry underfoot, outcrops of rock. I turn to look back. The sea is a long way down, a silver flatness shining in the sun. Below me, the thick green stuff I've emerged from looks like close-packed broccoli.

I keep climbing. I want to be on the bare rock right at the top, where you can see clear across to the other peaks and there is no sound.

It's never so good coming down. The sun was shining up there and the rock I sat down on for half an hour was almost too hot, but now I'm in the hill's shadow. Running down the slope would be easier, but the heather hides deep cuts where water lies, and if I get any speed up I won't be able to stop. It would be so embarrassing to be stuck up here with a broken ankle or something, waiting for the Mountain Rescue to find me. Search party, police alert, helicopter combing the moor with searchlights. And I'm not a tourist, there'd be no excuse. I haven't brought my phone, either. It would work up here, right enough, but it doesn't get a signal in the hill shadow so I don't bother.

I'm down on the forest path now, but still careful. It's steep, with thick roots across the path, and stones that can give way under your foot.

What was that?

I thought I saw something flit between the trees, a bit behind me, to my left. I glance back, but there's nothing. Was it a deer? Not likely at this time of the year. The does with fawns are up on the moors and the young stags are hanging around the villages where the tourists take photos of them and give them bits of sandwich. It's only in a hard winter that they come into the forest for any green stuff they can find.

There it is again. Somebody's up there, watching.

I stop again and put my hair back from my face to have a better look round.

Nothing. Turn back, go on. I must have imagined it.

No, I didn't.

I'm being followed.

The sky is still clear and pale above the trees, but it's deep shadow here, with dark masses of stuff like elder trees and hawthorn and bramble. Easy for someone to duck down and hide.

I go a bit faster. Not that I'm scared exactly. It's probably a sheep that's broken out of McAllister's field. The burn's low after these dry days, it could have paddled across. But it might be a human. Some boring person playing at Robin Hood who'll come trotting up all smiles and walk beside me, taking up too much space and doing tedious talking. I'm hurrying now. If I have to do the Robin Hood stuff, OK, it's time for a quick hide. Then I can see who it is and let them go past. There's a big Sitka spruce ahead, just past the bothy. I flatten myself behind it, hidden from whoever is coming. Good thing I'm skinny or bits of me would show round the edge. I twist my hair round my hand and hold it so it doesn't fly about.

Whoever's tracking me is moving quietly, but a twig snaps. He's getting nearer. Level with the tree now. I edge further round it so as to stay hidden and let him pass, but he stops. He's coming to look.

"Hi."

It's Kerry.

She's wearing the raggy shorts again, with a big black and brown patterned shirt that almost covers them. With her brown skin, she's like part of the forest. My heart's hammering against my ribs.

"I've followed you for ages," she says. "You're easy to see."

For the first time, I regret the orange hair. Or perhaps not.

She looks at me and frowns. "Sorry, it was just a game. Stupid, I guess. If you'd rather be on your own, that's OK. I'll go on."

"No! I mean – it's great."

Her eyes are very black in her dark face.

"I saw you duck behind the tree," she says.

And I thought I was being clever.

There's one of those silences.

I want to put my hand on her sleeve but I can't. I'm ashamed of the way I felt about her on the boat, as if she was something in a porn mag. I'm glad she doesn't know about that.

She's folded her arms, looking at me with her head on one side.

"You don't like people much, do you?" she says.

It's true, but I don't want to say that to her.

"I do sometimes. It's just – I don't like the thought of them. As a species, I mean."

It sounds nerdy and boring, the way I've put it, but she doesn't seem to mind. "Because of what we're doing to the planet?"

"Well – yes."

"Bad, isn't it. But you don't have to worry, people don't have it totally stitched up." She goes on, "Australia kills you pretty quick if you're not careful. Just a coupla weeks before we left, two guys ran out of petrol and they started to walk to the next place but it was too far and they didn't have enough water so they died on the roadside. Their dog, too. A truck driver saw them, lying there. Pity about the dog. The men should have known better, they were stupid."

She looks round at the trees and the burn.

"This is a good place, though. Plenty of shade, and there's water. Look at that ruined building. You could live in there."

She's picking up on stuff I've thought about for ages.

"It's a bothy," I say. "Like, a place to use when you're away from home, looking after animals."

But I need to explain what I mean about humans.

"It's not that I want people to die. At least, not right now. Some of them are OK. It's just – the stuff they do is so stupid. They go on like nothing's going to change. Making money, spending money, being important. And they do such awful things."

The pictures are back in my head again. Sick. "There's an e-mail going round, with photos of people in Denmark killing dolphins. I saw it last Monday. I mean, Denmark. They crack themselves up to be civilized. But there they were, wading around in the little bay where the dolphins come, waist-deep in blood, hacking them to death."

"Ah, shit," Kerry says.

It's been waking me at night.

"The dolphins scream. They make a noise like babies. It's only humans that can do stuff like that. I've heard people say foxes are bad because they kill more chickens than they need to eat, but they don't go out and conduct a fucking massacre for the fun of it."

"You're right," she says, in that Australian way that

sounds like *royt*. "It's totally out of order. Is there a petition or something?"

"Yeah. You're not supposed to sign petitions if you're under 18 but I did anyway."

"Send it on to me, I will too. I'll give you my address."

That's a plus, but I don't even stop to think about it.

"We're a mistake," I tell her. "We're an experiment that went wrong. But it can't go on. See, when the sea rises, the cities will be flooded because they're mostly built on rivers in the lowland. There'll be nothing to buy so money will be useless. People will start killing each other to grab a bit of what's left. They'll come here because of the hills and the way we can grow things and rear sheep. We'll have to fight. They'll make us into killers as well."

"You reckon?"

"Obvious, isn't it. But do they care? Do they even see it? All you get is the same old stuff. *Pass your exams, get a career, make money*. What's the point?"

I've never said all this to anyone before. Big risk. She'll tell all her pals I'm a nutter. But that's what they think anyway. Just because I'm not interested in the usual stuff. Buying smart gear, all that crap. Bob and Liam are OK. But we're in the band, and that's different.

Kerry's looking at me carefully.

She says, "D'you *need* a point?"

I feel like she's tripped me up. It's other people who have a point, not me.

"Seems to me it's OK just living," she goes on. "If you can't do anything about it, you might as well enjoy it while it lasts. Guess I'm the stupid kind."

"No! I didn't mean you, I was—"

She glances at her watch. "I'll have to go. Told them I'd be in by nine."

"I need to get back, too."

It's not true, but I want to stay with her.

She heads off down the path. I'm close behind. She's moving faster than I usually do, at a kind of half-run, re-laxed and easy. She's so fit. Pebbles slide from under my foot and I almost fall but I shift weight quickly and keep going. It's like I've found the same speed and balance that she has.

We're coming to the bothy where the path curves round to the other end of the village. The gate to the top of our garden is down to our right.

She stops and says, "That's your house, isn't it? The one down there."

"Yes. Listen, I'm sorry if I sounded kind of – depress-ing."

"No problem," she says. "Know how you feel. See you tomorrow, right?"

She sets off again. I watch until the trees hide her, but she doesn't look back.

Chapter 6

End-of-term concert. Hall packed with parents. We're thundering through the old Abba number, "Money, Money, Money." It's going pretty well. This is a scratch band, anyone Miss Irvine could round up, really. Liam and Bob are in it and there's Pat Lammas on flute and a couple of girls on clarinets and a third-year kid playing a xylophone, plus three other guitars and odd bits of extra percussion. It's hanging together because Liam and Bob are a solid rhythm section. Miss Irvine is conducting from the piano. She's such a good pianist, she can do anything, and keep everyone in order at the same time.

We get to the end of a chorus and she gives me a glance for a solo break. Great. I've been thinking of what to do. I put a double-time invention over the top, like tinkling coins, very fast and light. Not easy because it's all harmonics but I'm OK, I'm warmed up now. And bored enough with the rest of it to want to burst out a bit.

I get a hand for the solo and Miss Irvine smiles and nods. The whole band wades in for the final chorus.

Lots of applause at the end. Whistles, stamping – we're a bit amazed. It wasn't that good. We go off when the clapping dies down and I put the guitar on its stand, safe against the wall. I'm in again with the choir for the final number. I tried to duck it, but it's the mixed group and they're short of tenors so Miss Irvine asked if I would. We're doing "I Dreamed a Dream." Great tune. It's got the shiver factor.

OK, that's it wrapped up. Take a bow when Miss Irvine says. Clapping and stamping going on from the audience. The Head holds up his hand for silence – typical, he has to get into the act. Blah, blah, conventional thanks and stuff. Now he's thought of something else.

"Music of course is fortunate in that it can be easily heard and appreciated, but we should set that in the context of the rest of this school's work. Could we so readily appreciate the achievements being made every day in the fields of mathematics, science, technology and all the other subjects in our full range, we would truly be overwhelmed with richness. In our final thank you, I would like us to remember these other departments, unsung though they may be."

Pause for smirk.

"Please join me in appreciation of this school's work, whether audible or not."

If he was a horse, they'd shoot him. Talk about useless.

Everyone claps again, sort of, but he's broken the atmosphere and people are standing up and putting on their coats.

Kerry's pushing her way through the crowd. She's waving at me. So I wait.

She's reached the edge of the stage.

"That was *brilliant!*" she says. "I didn't know you were a musician. You never said."

She's wearing a green sparkly top over a short, frilly skirt. She looks amazing.

I crouch down with a hand on the floor, to be on her level.

"Glad you liked it."

How many times have I said that at the end of a gig and not meant it? But I mean it this time. She's so excited, she reaches her hand up to me and I grip it and hold it. We're both smiling like crazy.

"Well done," McCasky says from behind her. "Very good. See you in the car park."

"It was wonderful," adds Elaine. "You played so well."

Oh, get lost. But they mean well, I suppose.

"Be about five minutes," I tell them. "Is that OK?"

"Fine," McCasky says.

He and Elaine are both eyeing Kerry with interest.

"Catch you later," Kerry says to me.

She goes to join her mother, and they both look back

and wave as they go out. Her small brothers aren't here, and neither is their shaven-headed dad.

In the room behind the stage, people are shoving instruments into cases and wrapping up cables. Some of the girls are hugging each other.

"Nice solo, Cal," Miss Irvine says. "Tricky stuff, but you did it well."

"Thanks," I say.

Miss Irvine was new here last August. She's quite small, and wears long skirts and chunky ethnic necklaces, but she doesn't put up with any mucking about.

There's a kid making a mess of folding up a music stand. The bars will jam and get bent if he does it wrong, then the whole thing will be mucked up. I go over and sort him out.

"Look. Big ones up, little ones down."

"Thanks for that, Cal," Miss Irvine says when the kid's gone. Then she goes on, "You are going to take Music for Highers, aren't you?"

"Yeah. Think so."

"What do you mean, *think* so? You're a musician."

"I know, but—"

"Come on. It was bad enough when your sister went off to do rocket science or whatever. Don't say you're going to let me down as well."

"I'd really like to do music," I say. "It's just—"

I can't start telling her human beings are a disease. Not in two minutes. Not with Elaine and McCasky waiting outside.

"You think you ought to have a proper career?"

"I said I might do dentistry. I don't really want to, but—"

"But it makes money."

"Well, yes."

She sighs.

"Making money is fine if that's what turns you on. But there are other things. Personally, I'm allergic to boredom."

"Me too."

"For most people, work is a trade-off for cash," she goes on. "Nothing more. But it can be about finding what you've got in you and how to use it. Not an option if you don't have much. That's why so many people think artists and musicians and writers just muck about and enjoy themselves. They can't see that you have to be tough on yourself, dig out what you really want to express, never be satisfied until you've got it right. Being creative isn't an easy option. It's a hard, demanding business. But you wake up every morning a bit excited because it's what you want to do, there's all this interesting stuff waiting. It's the thing that really matters. Work as the great game."

"Yeah," I say. "That's right."

We're both smiling. If it was Jess, not my teacher, we'd thump fists, but the feeling is the same.

"So I want you here, doing music," Miss Irvine says. "Understand?"

Yes, of course I do. Talking to her, it all sounds so simple.

* * *

Elaine followed Fergus through the crowd, three paces behind him. She felt a bit as if she should have been wearing a burka, but he was good at the royal progress stuff, nodding at people he knew, clapping a friend on the shoulder, exchanging jokes. He was rude to his friends in a way they shared and enjoyed, and he didn't care about the others.

Someone close to her said, "Oh, hello."

She turned her head and found Andrew Duncan beside her, with Patsy and Ian Carradine and their two boys. Patsy gave Elaine a hug.

"Great to see you!"

Ian drifted ahead in the wake of his sons.

Patsy indicated her brother, still beaming. "Andrew *loved* his session with you last week," she said. "Didn't you, Andrew?"

Andrew smiled politely.

Elaine said, "That's nice," but she was a little surprised. He had never opened his eyes throughout the entire hour and a half, let alone made any comment.

"I think it was very useful," he said neutrally.

"I'm glad."

Patsy was rattling on. "Elaine, I'm running a half-marathon next month for Children in Need and I'm a bit bothered about my hamstrings. I need to put myself in for service. Can you fit me in next week?"

"Phone me tomorrow when I've got the appointments

book," said Elaine. "Then we can fix a time."

The crowd was thinning. Fergus had turned at the door, looking back to see where she was. He jabbed a finger in the direction of the car park. She waved to tell him she was coming.

"Must go," she said. "See you soon."

"Fine," said Patsy.

Andrew didn't say anything but, unexpectedly, he smiled at her.

"Quite a cookie you've got there," McCasky says over his shoulder as we're driving home. "Where's she from?"

"Australia."

"Yeah, but where else? Half-caste of some sort, isn't she. Aborigine or something?"

"I don't know. I've only just met her. She's not my girl-friend or anything."

"Soon will be," he says. "She's just waiting for the nod."

"Fergus, *really*," says Elaine. "That's no business of ours."

"Sorry I spoke," he says heavily.

Elaine witters on about how she liked what the choir sang and how good the evening was, but McCasky doesn't say anything else all the way home. By the time we get back, it's chucking it down with rain.

Still raining this morning. It's eased off, but the clouds are low over the hills and the air feels soupy, waiting for the sun to burn its way through again. It's break time and we're all in the reception area. Can't go out, the air's heaving with midges. It's horrible in here, it smells of people eating crisps and stuff.

I give Kerry a wave as I go past the group of girls she's with, and she comes to join me by the window.

"It was great last night," she says. "How long have you been playing?"

"I started in primary school."

She makes a face.

"We didn't get music in primary, only singing hymns and stuff."

"My father used to play a guitar," I tell her.

"Was he good?"

"Dunno, really. But he got me started."

He was OK then. Sometimes.

"I play a whistle," Kerry's saying. "We had an Irish music teacher in secondary school. He was into folk stuff. I never got to read music properly, but I can play any tune that comes into my head."

"Go on? We should have a session some time. Have you got your whistle in school?"

"No. I could bring it tomorrow, though."

"Great."

"When? Lunch break?"

I hadn't meant that soon, but there's no way I'll turn it down.

"OK. I'll ask Miss Irvine if we can use the music room."

Kerry does a thumbs-up sign. "See you there," she says.

Elaine's sitting at the kitchen table when I get in, but she gets up quickly and goes to the sink, runs the tap, splashes some water over her face, reaches for the towel.

She's been crying.

"Sorry," she says, sounding choked. "It's just – Barnaby's been killed."

"Oh, no."

Barnaby has always been her favourite, he was round her feet all the time or asleep on her lap.

"What happened?"

"He got under the wheels of the pick-up. Your dad – brought him in." She's in tears again. "He said he was sorry."

I put my arms round her. I'm upset, too. Barnaby was beautiful, black and brown stripes like a tiger. He didn't have a lot to do with me, he was Elaine's personal cat, but I liked looking at him and stroking him. Elaine's totally wrecked. She's weeping like a little kid. I just keep hugging her. There's nothing else I can think of that's any use.

After a bit she moves away and takes a tissue from the box.

"When did it happen?" I ask.

"About an hour ago. Your dad came in with something wrapped in a dust sheet. With dried plaster on it. Then I

saw it was Barnaby. His tail was hanging straight down."
She's fighting tears again.

"I'm really sorry."

McCasky comes in. It's still raining and he's fairly wet.
He goes to the sink and washes earth off his hands.

"Cup of tea, I think," he says.

He moves aside to let Elaine put the kettle under the
tap.

I go upstairs.

I'll e-mail Jess and ask her to phone Elaine when she
gets in. She'll know what to say.

I thought Kerry meant the short kind of whistle like the
piccolo in the Orange bands. I wasn't too keen, though I
didn't say so. They're so shrill. But she undoes the draw-
string on a leather bag and takes out a wooden pipe about
the size of a clarinet, only it doesn't have any keys. She
plays a quick ripple of notes up and down. It sounds a bit
breathy, but it's clear and warm, and there's a rich, smoky
tone at the bottom.

It's just her and me. I didn't mention it to Bob and
Liam, thought I'd check out whether she's any good first.
She starts on an Irish jig. The chord sequence is dead simple so I join in. It sounds OK but there's nothing much to
it.

"What else d'you do?" I ask at the end. "Something
blues-y?"

She thinks for a minute then says, "I know a lament. It's not blues, though."

She starts on a slow tune. Very minor, like a wordless song. It sends the shivers down my back, but it's hard to work out how to add anything.

"Do it again," I say when she gets to the end. So she does.

I put chords in here and there. She's right, it's too loose to be a blues. No heavy beat to it. Not American.

She says, "Think you could play the tune? I could put stuff with it."

I've not quite got the melody yet but I make up what I don't know and it kind of fits. She's doing a sort of *obbligato* over the top. It's starting to sound quite good.

Liam comes in. He must have heard from outside. He perches on a desk and listens.

"That's amazing," he says at the end. "Do you do anything else? Like, jazz or rock?"

"Never tried," Kerry says. "I'll have a go, though."

The school drum kit is in the corner. Liam gets his sticks from the cupboard and settles behind it.

"'Stairway to Heaven'?" he suggests.

He and I play through it a couple of times while Kerry listens. We've never played it without Jess, so I'm having to do the melody. It sounds thin on the guitar.

Kerry starts to join in. She's got the feel of it. The sound she makes is very different from the sax, but it kind of works.

At the end, Liam says to me, "She's a bit quiet, but we could mic her."

"Why not?" I say.

And the bell goes. That's the trouble with school, you just get stuck into something and you have to stop.

Kerry comes to sit beside me on the bus.

"My mum says there's an Iron Age fort up the hill," she says. "She used to go up there when she was a kid, but then they planted the trees and nobody could get to it. D'you know where it is?"

I thought she'd want to talk about music, but this is something else.

"Yeah," I tell her. "You'd have passed it on the way down when you tracked me that evening. People made such a fuss about it being planted over, the Forestry cut the trees down after a year or two and cleared the site."

"Will you show me?" she says.

Will you show me! I haven't had to ask her, she's asking me. I feel warm all over but I try to sound casual.

"Sure. Weekend maybe?"

"That would be great. Phone me when you're free. I'll give you my number."

I tap the digits into my phone.

"OK," I say, trying to sound like this happens all the time. "I'll call you."

Chapter 7

Elaine heaved the last bag into her trolley at the checkout. Joanie Barr at the till handed her the folded length of receipt and her card from the machine and asked, "You all right?"

"Oh ... yes, fine." She hadn't spoken to Joanie or arranged her face to look cheerful. "Sorry. I was thinking of something else." She managed a smile.

She was still in that moment of taking Barnaby from Fergus, a wrapped weight of heavy stillness that seemed already cold, though he couldn't have been. His eyes had been wide open, but they were chalky white and stared at nothing.

Fergus had said, "I'll go and dig a hole."

She had spread a newspaper on the floor and laid Barnaby down very gently as if he could be further hurt, then washed her hands because there was blood on them. Jingle had come in through the cat-flap, taken one aghast look and fled out again.

The scene was replaying itself again as she pushed her trolley out from beside the till, and she unseeingly let it bump into a man's ankle.

"I'm so sorry," she said.

She put her hand over her forehead, trying to hold everything together. *Mustn't cry here, in front of everyone.*

The man had turned, he was going to be annoyed, couldn't blame him.

"Elaine," he said. "Hello."

Andrew Duncan.

Elaine shook her head slightly. She couldn't do the professional thing right now. But he was looking concerned.

"I was so sorry to hear about your cat," he said.

She hadn't expected that. Words wouldn't come. To her huge embarrassment, her eyes were filling with tears. She looked away, struggling.

"Let me take your trolley."

He added his own full bag to it and steered for the door.

"Where are you parked?" he asked over his shoulder.

"By that tree."

He loaded her stuff into the boot of the Polo. "Don't go," he said. "I'll be right back."

Elaine leaned against the car, stupidly glad to be taken charge of. Vaguely, she saw him put his shopping in his own car and shunt the trolley into the line of others. He came back and gave her the pound coin from it.

"Could you use a quiet coffee somewhere?" he asked.

"Say no if you'd rather be alone. I won't be offended."

She didn't want to be alone. *That's the whole trouble, being so alone.*

"I'd like to," she said.

She walked beside him out of the car park, and he remarked, "Such a risk with cats. But they have to have their freedom."

"Yes."

Fergus could have been more careful, though. He always came into the yard too fast.

"Was he your only cat?"

"No, there's Jingle. But he's a hunter so he's out a lot." *I mustn't be unfair to him.* "And yet, an hour later, he came in and leaned his head against me."

"People think cats don't understand," Andrew said. "But they do."

In the cafe he saw her to a table in the corner then went to the counter to give the order. A couple sitting by the window smiled across at Elaine and said, "Lovely day!"

"Wonderful."

She couldn't remember their names. So many people knew her by sight, Fergus McCasky's wife. She studied the menu unseeingly. She knew what they'd be talking about. There were rumours all over the island about the firm being in trouble. And her presence in here with some other man wasn't going to help.

To hell with them.

She sat back, too tired to pretend.

Andrew put the coffees down carefully and slid into the chair opposite her.

"There's a biscuit," he said, indicating the very small wrapped wafer in the saucer. "Comes with it."

"Yes. Thank you."

After a bit she asked, "How did you know about Barnaby?"

"Patsy told me. There's a kid who's in the same class as her older boy. His mum works for your husband."

Maggie Lawson.

Andrew's grey eyes were regarding her steadily.

"You're really wiped out, aren't you," he said. It wasn't a question.

"A bit."

Admitting to it nearly started her crying again. *It's everything else, not just Barnaby.* But she couldn't start on all that. Unprofessional. Andrew was a client.

"Silly to be so upset," she said.

"Not silly at all," said Andrew. "You're still in shock. It's always like that. Easy enough while things have to be done, you just get on with it. Then the reaction and the exhaustion." He smiled apologetically. "Why am I telling you? You're the expert."

She thought again of lifting the towel from his chest in the warm treatment room and seeing the healed but still shocking injury. She wasn't the expert at all. He'd been through things she couldn't start to imagine.

"Why don't you pack in this therapy stuff?" Fergus said that night. "It takes a lot out of you. And for what you make, you'd be better giving me a hand in the office."

It wasn't the first time he'd mentioned that. Unfair to bring it up again now, when she felt so weak at the knees. But Fergus always pushed his advantage.

"Come on, Elaine, why don't you think about it?" he said. "Maggie Lawson barely earns her money, she's a lazy cow. Dumping her would be a big saving."

"So I'd work for nothing."

He shook his head irritably. "You'd be working for *us*. The firm is what we all live on. It's a bad time for the building trade, you know that. Orders cancelled, houses standing unsold."

"The papers say the worst of it is over," Elaine said.

"Like hell it is. If I don't cut expenses I'll go to the wall. A downturn is the best time to invest, but you can't get the silly buggers to see that."

"No, I suppose not."

She was fending him off as usual, trying to find something to agree about, but panic was close. Fergus wanted to take away her freedom, her professional life, her usefulness, everything that made her a person of some value. She floundered for an excuse.

"I'd be letting so many people down," she said, then saw the chance she had given him.

He pounced on it. "You don't mind letting *me* down."

"I've never let you down. I never would. I fit the therapy sessions around everything else."

"You could fit the office work around *everything else*," said Fergus. Then he switched to straight appeal. "Elaine, look, I need someone reliable in the office. You'd be useful."

"But – I *am* useful. It's just, in a different way."

And to different people, of course. That's the trouble.

Fergus pushed his chair back. "The way things are now, you're as much use to me as a wet lettuce leaf. I'm going to bed, I've work to do in the morning."

Elaine heard his heavy footsteps go up the stairs and into their room. A drawer was opened then pushed shut. *Clean clothes for the morning.* This wasn't the first time. The footsteps went across the landing to Jess's room, empty now she wasn't here, and the door slammed.

I must change the sheets before Jess comes home, Elaine thought bleakly. *She won't be here long, just to pack for Malaysia. But I don't want her to know.*

Loneliness filled the room. She turned the television on for the sake of its empty company.

"They picked a good place, didn't they," Kerry says.

She's standing at the edge of the Iron Age site where the land falls away, staring across the top of the trees, both hands shading her eyes against the sun.

"You can see for miles," she goes on. "They'd know if any boats were coming. It's brilliant."

I want her to stop talking about Iron Age people. I want her to turn round and look at me. Really look, not just at the space I happen to occupy. But I don't know what I'd do if she did. So I go on mooching about, stamping down bracken fronds. Horrible stuff, it smothers everything. It was all right when the cattle were out on the hill, they trod it down, but they have to be turned into beef when they're very young these days, so there's no time for that sort of thing.

All I've made is a silence. OK, Iron Age, if that's what we've got to talk about.

"They had signal fires. They lit them if invaders came."

"And then what?"

"The women took the kids somewhere safe and the men went out to fight."

"That's a bum idea," she says. "The guys are killed off and the women get raped by Vikings or whoever."

No point in arguing. I sit down on a flat slab of stone that used to be a house roof all those years ago. It's warm in the sun. Ants underneath it. They fight marauders and keep their young ones safe. We will, too, if we ever stop ruining the world. My head is in my hands.

"What's the matter?" Kerry asks.

I don't answer. I squint at her against the sun but I can't see her properly, it's too dazzling, she's just a dark shape.

She comes and sits on the flat stone as well, with a space between us. My hair is over my face and I don't bother pushing it back.

She says, "You don't want me here, do you?"

My head jerks up.

"I do. Of *course* I do—"

But she's leapt to her feet. She's screaming and brushing at her bare legs and jumping about like a lunatic. What on earth—

"Ants!" she shrieks. "Aaargh! Get them off me!"

That's ridiculous.

"They won't hurt you," I say.

She's still brushing and hopping, but she pauses.

"You sure?"

"Yeah. They're running over me, too, look." I show her a couple of ants on my wrist. "They can probably smell the apples."

"What apples?"

"There are two in my pocket."

She brushes another ant off. She's still moving about uneasily, picking her feet up and shaking them. She goes to sit on the wooden bench near the trees that are left, tucking her feet up and still inspecting her arms and legs. She's kicked her sandals off. I go to join her.

"In Australia we've got fire ants," she says. "Their bites make you feel like there's acid on your skin. If there's a lot of them, they can kill you."

"Good reason for not living there," I say, but she's still cross.

"Fire ants aren't Australian. They came in on the ships."

"Without tickets?"

It takes her a second to realize it's a joke, then she thumps me on the knee, really hard. I grab her wrist. She tries to break my grip but I put the other hand on. Next minute, we're into a full-scale wrestle, still on the bench but with feet jammed against the ground, pushing and shoving for advantage. She's very strong, she's fighting me like she's furious but I don't know what she's got to be furious about, I'm the one who's having a bad time, thinking about her the whole time and getting treated like I was thin air. I've got both her wrists now and I cross them in front of her chest, pushing her away. She's nearly off the edge of the bench and she gives a squeak of fear that I'll push her over.

What am I doing? This is crazy.

I let go of her wrists very carefully, one at a time, with my head ducked in case she hits me, and help her up.

"Sorry," I say. "I'm really sorry. That was stupid."

Her shoulders are hunched.

"Oh, shit," she says tiredly.

I'm terrified I've hurt her.

"Kerry. Are you all right?"

She doesn't answer. She turns to me and sighs. The next minute, her face is against my shoulder and her arms are round my neck and somehow mine are round her.

"I'm so sorry," I say again. And my fingers push through her curly hair the way I've dreamed of, and I can feel the warm hardness of her head under my palm. She turns her face up to mine and our mouths are finding each other. Finding. Found.

After a bit she pushes my hair back with both hands. She holds it there while she looks at me, really looks at me. In the sun, I can see that her black eyes have coppery flecks in them, though the pupils are so dark that I can't imagine the thoughts behind them.

"I've wanted to do this ever since I first saw you," she says. "That time on the boat."

"Me too. I've been dreaming about you."

We both laugh, kind of breathlessly.

I trace a finger down her nose and across her upper lip and she opens her mouth like a baby bird, gently taking my finger between her teeth. Then she lets go and pulls my head close again.

"How have you been?" says Pirelli. "Had a good week?"

I can't help smiling. Not just good, it's been amazing, the two of us meeting every day after school and pretty well all weekend. The hill is our territory now, those places we've been to, special to just us.

Pirelli smiles back. "*That* good?" he says. "I'm really glad. Any special reason?"

I want to tell him. I want to tell everyone, I want to

dance round lampposts like Gene Kelly in *Singing in the Rain*, but that would blow the secret. It's not for anyone else, it's ours. And it's more than secret – it's a kind of wild magic.

Pirelli just waits like he always does. He's never pushed a lot of stupid questions, he's been good that way, and I've never told him anything much. He deserves a break.

"I met someone really nice," I say.

"Congratulations," he says.

But he leaves a space again, and I feel I ought to fill it, even though I don't have to.

So I tell him, "It's like, whatever I think of, she's thought of it, too."

"I know what you mean," he says. "It's great when you've interests in common."

Oh, yes. We've these interests in the touch and smell and sound of each other. The feel of each other. It's the hobby to end all hobbies. But I suppose he means stuff like stamp collecting. And if he doesn't, it's a step too far to tell him.

"We're both into music," I say, a bit breathless because of what I'm not saying. "She plays the Irish whistle."

"Maybe you've found a new band member?"

"Could be."

But Bob and Liam aren't that impressed, except by the way she looks. Bob said afterwards, "She's not much of a player, but we could do some fantastic publicity photos."

Then he asked if she was my bird, but I said she wasn't.

Pirelli says, "Do you like drawing?"

"It's OK."

He slides a stack of paper across to me, all different colours, and a mug with felt tips in, and says, "Take your pick."

"What d'you want me to draw?"

"Happiness," he says.

If he thinks I'm going to draw Kerry and me, tough. He can mind his own business. So I go through the sheets of paper, looking at the colours and faffing about with the felt tips.

Pirelli's filling in forms. All right for some, getting paid to talk to nutters like me and do the paperwork at the same time. Cheek, really.

The only thing that came anywhere near meeting Kerry was the golden eagles. I was up on the hill last summer and there were these two eagles, doing a kind of air dance. They were high up, hard to see because the sun was so bright. I lay flat in the heather with my hands shading my eyes so I could watch them without getting a crick in my neck. Their massive wings cut great patterns in the air, then they'd fold them and dive, the two of them together like they were one thing, dropping like a huge stone, and at the last minute they parted and soared up and started the dance all over again. It was brilliant.

I don't know how to draw eagles. No point in trying to

get them to look right. Pirelli can Google them if he wants to know what they're like. The great thing about them was the pattern they were making in the air. So I draw that with a pale blue felt tip, then put in black things for the eagles and a blaze of yellow for the sun. It looks like something by a five-year-old. You wouldn't know what size the birds were or anything. So I add a pink and purple scribble along the bottom for heather and draw a boy lying flat like I was, small compared with the eagles. It's getting quite interesting.

Pirelli looks at his watch.

"That's about our lot for today," he says, then cocks his head to look at the drawing. He seems surprised. "Hey – you didn't tell me you're an artist."

"I'm not."

"But they're eagles, aren't they? Or huge birds of some sort."

"Well, yes. I saw them last summer."

"Great to live in a place like that," he says. "I must try to get over there some time."

He tucks the drawing into a plastic folder.

Somehow I don't want to leave it with him. It's mine. I want to show it to Kerry. He seems to know what I'm thinking. He takes it out and looks at it again, then hands it to me.

"Tell you what – I'll take a photocopy. Then you can keep the original."

"OK. Thanks."

We go down to the office and a secretary does a photocopy. Pirelli says, "Now, you do know this is the last session for the time being?"

I'd forgotten. I suppose it said in the letter, but I hadn't looked.

"We start again in September. I'll be there for the first session, but after that you'll be with someone else. Janet, she's called. She's very nice. You'll like her."

"Aren't you coming back, then?"

"I'm getting married, actually." He smiles. It's the same kind of smile I had when I said I'd had a good week. "My wife-to-be is head of a primary school in Lancashire, so we'll be living down there."

He's as smug as a cat with the cream. Don't know why I feel so miffed, but I do. And if he thinks I'm starting all over again with some woman called Janet, he's wrong.

Chapter 8

Kerry's doing the lead on whistle. Bob and Liam are playing. It's almost like *Sign On*, but different. We've always been into classic rock, but this is more like away with the fairies.

It's after school, but Miss Irvine's come to listen.

"I think that's really interesting," she says at the end. "I love the breathy tone."

"Bit folky," Bob says.

I've got a text message from Jess.

jst off boat me & mairi coming to school with her mum c u soon

I shouldn't have told her we were having a practice. I know what she's up to – she wants to meet Kerry. And Mairi is tagging along. Oh, shit. Now I'll have to go home with Jess in Mairi's mum's car instead of on the bus with Kerry. We were going to go up the hill but that's blown.

Miss Irvine asks, "Kerry, do you sing?"

Kerry shakes her head. "Not really. I was in the choir at school, but it was "Waltzing Matilda" and stuff."

"Do you know a different sort of music?"

"Kinda. But – people might not like it."

"Australian music? Aboriginal?"

"Well, yeah. My mum used to take me to the Koori museum, and musicians came there sometimes."

"Can you do some?"

"Yeah. But it's a bit weird."

"Can we try? What do we need?"

"Nothing much. They use clapsticks, but a drum would do."

"What speed?" asks Liam.

"Fairly quick – it just keeps going."

"Give it a try," says Bob. "What d'you want on the bass?"

"Same thing over and over."

She sings a short phrase, just a rise and fall, but rhythmic. Bob picks it up and Liam joins in. I put in a repeated chord, quite a hard sound.

We get the riff going and Kerry nods, clicking her fingers to it, thinking.

She starts making short sounds. Not singing, more like some kind of wild dog yapping. Dead right it's weird. She moves into a kind of chattering, like birds. Liam and Bob and I keep the background rhythm steady. What she's doing gets more complicated, with long howls and a kind of talking. We don't change, just hang on in there with the same backing. She starts thinning the chant out again, like it's all going away, and brings it to an end.

"Wow!" says Jess from the door. "That's fantastic!"

Mairi and her mother are looking gobsmacked but Miss Irvine is really excited.

"Are there other forms, Kerry?" she asks. "Different rhythm patterns?"

"There's all sorts," Kerry says. "Men do the singing mostly."

"Don't women sing *anything*?" Jess asks, like she can't believe it.

"Well, yeah. But their songs are different. Kinda – slower."

Miss Irvine says, "Can we try one?"

"Could do."

Kerry frowns, thinking about it. She begins to click her fingers again, but carefully, setting a beat so slow that it's leaning on the need for another one in between. When we've got it going, she starts singing long phrases in a language I don't understand. I'm not sure she understands it, either, but I guess she remembers this music from when she was a kid.

It's not like the other song. It gives me the shivers. There's something ancient and sad about it, like someone is telling about things that are really hard. But it's beautiful, too. There's no way to work out what key Kerry's in. Bob's got a riff going on a low A-flat that he comes back to all the time, but the harmony doesn't work in any way that I know. I just have to find notes that fit what Kerry's doing. She's leaving gaps between the sung phrases, and I look at her in case she'd like bits of solo guitar as a kind of echo. She gives me a nod.

We keep going. It's starting to work well.

The voice on the PA cuts through.

THE SCHOOL WILL BE CLOSING IN FIVE MINUTES.

So we glance at each other and shrug, and wind down to a stop.

"Kerry, that's wonderful," Miss Irvine says. She's looking totally spaced out, as if she can't believe the music she's heard. "It's like a Celtic lament, only – not Celtic. Quite extraordinary."

"The slow ones are called Ngathi," Kerry tells her. "Yeah, they are laments, but this one's a love song, too."

Miss Irvine smiles and shakes her head.

"That was no ordinary love song," she says.

Jess comes over to join us.

"Hi," she says to Kerry, "I'm Cal's sister. That's really special, Kerry. You lot could do a terrific crossover thing. World music as modern jazz, know what I mean?"

Bob looks across from unplugging his amp and nods. "Yeah," he agrees. "Made for it."

Kerry puts her whistle in its leather bag and pulls the tie-string tight. She smiles at Jess, but it's like she's thinking about something else.

"I'm going for the bus," she says, and heads for the door.

"We can give you a lift," Jess calls after her.

"'S all right."

And she's gone.

Up in my room, Jess puts "Dark Side of the Moon" on. She's into modern jazz really but she still likes the classics. Or she's picked what she knows I'll like. Maybe I'm stupid, but the old music seems kind of – secure or something. They knew what they meant, it's not just technical showing-off.

"So you've got yourself a girlfriend," Jess says.

I frown. How does she know? We were just playing music.

"Come on," Jess says. "You can't imagine it's a secret. The way she looked at you says it all. It's great. I'm really happy for you."

Pink Floyd is filling the room. Roger Waters was a genius. *Breathe, breathe in the air, don't be afraid to care, leave but don't leave me.* I'm seeing it in a different way now.

Jess is sprawled on my bed. She chucks me a tube of Polo mints. I take one and chuck it back. She gets one out for herself then holds it up and looks at it. Small, white, with a hole in the middle. I know what she's going to say.

"How's your tyre man?"

"He's going to get married," I say. "So that's the end of that."

"Oh, right. Well, guess you're more cheerful now."

Now you've got Kerry, she means. I've always shared

everything with Jess, but she's looking at me a bit narrow-eyed and I feel uneasy.

"Kerry's older than you, isn't she."

"Not much. Eight months."

I don't see why she's asking.

"Is there a law that says your girlfriend has to be younger than you?"

"'Course not."

But she's frowning.

"Look, Cal, I know it's not my business, but Mairi's mum works for the home care people. She gives a hand looking after Kerry's grandmother. Gets her lunch, that sort of thing. And the old lady likes to talk about her family, the way old people do."

And Mairi's mum likes passing it on. Charming.

"So?"

"Well – Kerry had an affair in Australia when she was quite young, with a much older guy. Her parents were really worried."

"And you think I need to know this?'

"Yes, I do," Jess says. "You're going to hear it from someone, sooner or later. And I don't want to know something that concerns you and not tell you. It doesn't seem right."

"What about you and Mark McKitterick, then?"

Jess was only fifteen and Mark had a wife and kid. Mc-Casky went round and sorted him out.

"That's just what I mean," Jess says. "So if I ever meet

someone I seriously like, I'll tell him about Mark before anyone else does."

I'm annoyed. Kerry would have told me about the other bloke when she wanted to. And Jess is wrong, anyway, I don't want to know there was someone else. Someone else's hands, someone else's mouth – the Polo mint is still spreading its sweetness across my tongue, but I feel a bit sick.

"Ah, come on," says Jess. "I didn't mean to upset you, but it's the way things are. Look at our parents, for goodness' sake."

"What about them?"

"They're not getting on well, are they. Pop's been sleeping in my room. I know, because his clock's on my bedside table. I guess Elaine mistook it for mine. She's done a pretty good job otherwise, except she went over the top with the air freshener. In case I got a whiff of stinky socks."

"Could be because he snores or something."

Jess shakes her head. "He's got someone else, I bet you. It's happened before."

Jess knows about a whole lot of stuff that I never even think of. I'm like a meercat or something, out of the burrow for a quick look around and back in again, but she's up there in a different world. When we were eating tonight she was giving McCasky a rundown of the Glasgow flats she thinks are possible, and next week she's off to Kuala Lumpur. Then back to Glasgow to start uni. She just – does things. Gets on.

She's smiling again.

"Have another Polo mint," she says.

Elaine was vacuuming the hall when Andrew came to the door. She saw his silhouette through the stained glass and switched the machine off before he'd rung the bell.

"Hi," she said, smiling. "Come in."

His casual droppings-in had become a kind of random bonus, never to be depended on but always refreshing and a little surprising.

"If you're not too busy," he said with his usual courtesy.

She smiled again. He never took her for granted.

"Don't be silly," she said. "Mind the vacuum cleaner."

He stepped over its hose and followed her into the kitchen.

"Tea, coffee, herbal?" she offered.

"Just water," he said. "Pretty hot out there."

Elaine put a chunk of lemon and an ice cube in each glass, then ran the water cold before she topped them up. "Cooler in here than the conservatory," she said, and he nodded. They sat down at the table.

Andrew drank briefly then set the glass down and folded his arms over the large white envelope he had brought with him.

"Elaine," he said, "I want to make an outrageous proposition."

"Go on?" she said.

She didn't bother wondering what he meant. Lunch out, perhaps. A trip to a concert. He was wearing a pale blue shirt with the sleeves rolled up. His arms were very suntanned now. She knew his chest and back were much less brown.

He took a deep breath.

"Elaine," he said. "Forgive this if it's an impertinence, but I feel you need a break."

She made a rueful face, agreeing but offering no comment.

"And if I read the situation right," he went on, "you're not going to get one."

"It's difficult for Fergus," she said in wifely defence. "He needs to buy a flat for Jess in Glasgow because if Callum goes to university as well it will be much cheaper in the long run, but houses aren't moving. If he could just get one sale—"

Andrew cut through her flurry of words.

"You can't help him with that." He was looking at her steadily. "You know what you've taught me through these sessions?"

She shook her head. Not for the first time, she imagined running her fingers down the pitted skin of his face and suppressed the thought quickly. Faces were personal. They belonged in dreams. Certainly not in professional reality.

"You made it clear that it's no crime to take care of yourself," Andrew said. "People like you and me, we slog on, doing something because it's a job that needs to be done and nobody else can do it. But we wear ourselves thin. We're like drivers who never put the car in for maintenance then wonder why it fails its MOT."

She couldn't disagree, she'd said the same thing so many times to stressed and overburdened people.

"Yes," she said.

He sat back and slid a brochure out of the white envelope.

"Look," he said, and pushed it across to her.

Blue sky, olive trees.

"This is a course called Giving Back," he said. "It's not cranky as far as I can see. They offer rest and food and various therapies, but you don't have to live on carrot juice and meditation. In fact, the food sounds rather good. And there's plenty of time to do your own thing."

Elaine looked at the pictures. She'd need her glasses to read the text beside them, but there was no point in discovering the details – this was fantasy. White walls, a riot of scarlet flowers. A little boy leading a donkey. A cool room with pale curtains, the sun outside. Did he really think she could go to this place? She almost wept with longing. But she shook her head.

"Hang on," said Andrew. "I haven't got to the outrageous bit yet." He took a deep breath. "Elaine, listen. I salted away a good bit of money when I was working, and did sensible things about insurance. Paying for this will be no problem. The thing is, I don't want to go on my own.

What I'm suggesting is that you come away with me for two weeks – or more – as my guest."

She laughed breathlessly.

"And how do I explain that to Fergus?"

"I suggest you tell him you have been invited to run a course," Andrew said with perfect gravity. "A client of yours who went to this place told them all about you and gave them your details. They're short-handed because of a staff death or what have you, so they phoned to ask if you can help them out. They'll pay you. It will cost Fergus no money."

It sounded so reasonable that Elaine found herself considering it as though it were possible. Which, of course, it was not. She laughed again and said, "You're a brilliant liar."

"Let's say I'm creative," Andrew said. "Good at constructing scenarios."

Elaine looked down again at the brochure.

"It's impossible, of course," she said. "But if it was in any way real – when would you be thinking of?"

"That's up to you," he said, "but the actual departure will happen at short notice, as far as anyone else is concerned. Replacement staff are always needed instantly. That's the nature of emergencies. But the date of this emergency is your choice."

She nodded slowly. The idea was outrageous, as Andrew said, but her very bones ached for it.

"So you'll come?" he asked.

Count to three, she told herself. *Slowly. Let reality kick in.* But the thrill of it wouldn't let her count, the numbers were dancing about and she stopped trying to control them.

She put her hands over her face.

"I think – I really might," she heard herself say.

Andrew smiled and said, "That's my girl."

The old-fashioned phrase enchanted her even more, and the dream reached out to overcome all good sense. She put her fingers to the side of his face at last and slid them down the pitted skin to the angle of his jaw. And he leaned forward and kissed her.

"Cal," says McCasky. "How's it going?"

He's caught me coming down the garden from the top gate. No escape.

"OK," I say.

"Come into the office," he says. "Too hot to talk out here."

No argument about that. It's sweltering and heavy, as if there's going to be a storm. I follow him across the yard into the office he built beside the car park, backing onto his big store that sells timber and DIY stuff.

In the outer office where Maggie Lawson and Mrs Bowker fall silent at the sight of him he opens the glass door of the drinks fridge and takes out a can of beer. "Pepsi?" he asks.

I nearly say no, but I'm hot and thirsty.

"Thanks."

He nods like he appreciates the word and hands me

the cold can. I follow him into his office. He slides into his big chair behind his desk and switches the fan on. I sit the other side of his desk. I've a nasty feeling this is a job interview. I told him I meant to keep on at school, but that's ended. We've six weeks now before term starts again.

He plunges straight in. "These holidays. We can't go anywhere this year. Things are bad, and I've a lot of expense. Your sister's off to Malaysia, but she's earned the money for the fare and Caroline will take care of her. But you're something else."

I can see what's coming. I need to work. Kerry's got a job. She's working at her dad's outdoor shop.

"Yes," I say.

"Steve's due four weeks off, he's been saving his holiday leave to go to Canada. So Bill's on his own in the store. He can't do that and the deliveries. What I'm suggesting is, I pay you as a trainee. It's not a bad place to work. Better than some greasy cafe. And you won't find much else now – the kids who were quick off the mark got the pick of the jobs."

I nod.

"Let me spell this out," he says. "I don't mind giving you pocket money while you're at school, I count that as a job. But if you think I'm paying you to run around on the hill with your Aussie girlfriend, you can think again."

Jeez – does *everyone* know?

"So make up your mind," he says. "What's it to be?"

No choice.

"When do I start?"

"Monday," he says. "Up, breakfasted and ready to go by half past eight. Right?"

"Right."

McCasky hands me a red T-shirt with the firm's name across it.

"Stick that on," he says.

It's covered with dried splashes of yellow paint but I don't mind. At least I won't look like I'm new on the job. Bill Cowall is putting a box of cheap Chinese pliers on the edge of the counter with a notice, £1.99. He's worked here for years. He looks up and sees me and my red shirt and orange hair and grins. He's got terrible teeth.

"You look like a bonfire," he says.

Red shirt, yellow splashes, orange hair. Yeah, suppose so.

McCasky says. "Don't take this wrong, but you'd be safer in here if you tie your hair back. You don't want it catching on stuff. They'll have a rubber band in the office."

"OK."

It's not worth arguing.

"Everything's price-marked," he goes on. "And bar-coded. No discounts for your mates, right? It'll show up on the till and I'll knock it off your wages."

"Right."

"The stuff out the back's different," he says. "That's not new stock."

He means the bit behind the fence where scrap gets dumped. Half rolls of roofing felt, junk timber, plumbing bits.

"I don't mind if you do someone a favour," he goes on. "A quid from some old biddy who wants a few bricks to edge a flower bed, OK. Anything more, ask me."

"OK."

He glances at his watch then says to Bill, "I'm due in Colbeag. Keep him busy."

"Sure," says Bill, and gives me his grotty grin again. "Slave-driving starts here."

The place seems more cheerful than I'd expected.

McCasky goes out to his pick-up and Bill says, "I'll show you where everything is, then you'll have some idea what you're doing. You'll need the code for the card machine but that can wait."

He starts down the avenue of paints and white spirit. I've been in here before so I know the layout roughly, but I don't mind looking interested.

We get to the rows of boxes and he says, "Nuts – screws, washers and bolts. Like the escaped lunatic in a laundry. Nails loose by the kilo. Sanders, drills, angle grinders. Spare blades and disks."

A woman comes in and says, "Have you got anything to stick a handle on a jug? It's a really nice jug but my daughter came to visit and she knocked it against the tap when she was doing the washing up. I wish people wouldn't wash up, really, they never do it properly, but you know what they're like."

Bill leads her off to the adhesives. I tag along to watch.

The woman settles for two tiny Superglue tubes in a blister pack, £4.99.

"It should work," Bill says as he hands her the penny change from a fiver. "Only don't lift it up full of hot water, will you."

"Oh, no," she says. "I only want it to put flowers in."

When she's gone, Bill says, "She could have bought a new jug for that."

I quite like him, really. I wish he'd do something about the teeth, though. They make him look such an old wreck.

It's Sunday morning. We're all in the kitchen, gobsmacked. Elaine says she's going to Greece. McCasky is sitting in a heavy silence, and she's looking flustered.

"I won't be away for very long," she says. "I'll leave stuff in the freezer. I do hope you'll be all right."

I say, "We won't. You'll find my starved corpse on the floor."

It was meant to be funny but she just looks unhappier.

"Where is this place, exactly?" McCasky asks.

"It's a small island near Corfu. I forget what it's called, Greek names are so difficult. There's an agent in London who's fixing the travel and everything."

Jess is listening with her arms folded. She's off to stay with Caro in Malaysia in two days' time.

"And how did you hear about it, exactly?" she asks.

"Like I say, one of my clients had been there. And they were desperate for help, their therapist had left. So she gave them my number, just in case I was interested, and they phoned. They sound very nice."

I can see Jess thinks it's odd.

"But you don't have their e-mail address or anything?"

"No," says Elaine. She's in fighting mouse mode, talking fast. "I'm not sure they have e-mail. I think it's quite remote. It won't cost anything. They'll pay me. And – I've always wanted to go to Greece, it looks so beautiful."

McCasky says, "Well, don't do it for peanuts. What are they offering?"

Elaine looks flustered.

"It depends how many hours I work."

She's hopeless about money. If someone doesn't pay for a treatment session, she never chases them up properly.

McCasky glances at her, then sets his empty coffee mug on the table. "If you want to go, then go," he says. He levers himself to his feet, opens the kitchen door and walks across the yard to the office.

"I feel awful about it," Elaine says.

Jess looks at her in the same way that McCasky did.

"That's stupid," she says. "Dad's right. If you're going, then enjoy it. Have a great time."

Elaine doesn't notice the sarcasm. Or if she does, she's pretending not to.

"I suppose so," she says. She gets to her feet, not

looking at Jess or me, and picks up her basket. "There's such a lot of French beans – a pity to waste them. I'll put them in the freezer."

Jess turns to me when Elaine's gone out and says, "What *is* she up to?"

I shrug. Can't start to imagine. One of her whale music people suggested it, I suppose.

"Lousy timing from your point of view," Jess says. "With me off to Malaysia as well. If I'd known, you could have come with me."

I shake my head. "I don't like it there much. So hot and sweaty."

When I was there we spent most of the time in shopping malls, buying stuff. They overdid the air-conditioning and it was quite chilly.

"It's only hot outside," Jess says. "I'll be in the office with Caro mostly, and the building's air-conditioned. She's a computer designer – makes 3D prototype parts through a program that builds directly in plastic. It'll be so useful for my course."

I don't answer. She knows what I think about her doing that stuff instead of music.

She goes back to the subject of our mother.

"I can't believe Elaine would go traipsing off to Greece all on her own. If you ask me, she's met someone."

"Nah," I say. "Impossible."

Nobody could seriously fancy Elaine, with that straggly

grey hair and everything. It makes my toes curl to think about it.

"Oh, I don't know. Some handsome Greek pipsqueak?"

Can't resist it.

"Turk burk."

"Wes the Fez."

"Zeno Cappucino—"

"—met a feta cheese, yes, please."

Words are more fun than real thinking.

Jess went three days ago. And Elaine left this afternoon. She's staying in the airport hotel overnight, flying early tomorrow.

I'm sitting here playing my guitar, quietly. I don't want McCasky to come raging in saying is this going on all night some of us have got to get some sleep. I've been mucking about with Kerry's Irish thing, trying to find a good arrangement for it. Difficult without making it too complicated. And I can't remember how the Australian stuff goes.

I give up.

It's dark outside. The old Beatles number comes to mind. *Blackbird singin' at the dead of night...* I tune the bass string down and start playing it. McCasky likes that one.

Take these broken wings and learn to fly.

All my life,

I have just been waiting for this moment to arrive.

* * *

A plane with a tail-fin design from some foreign airline she'd never heard of travelled slowly along the tarmac outside the windows and Elaine was hit by cold horror. *What am I doing?* She sat back from her coffee and shut her eyes, trying to reason with herself. *They'll be all right.* She'd left the freezer stocked with food to put in the microwave, most of it made by herself in a week of frantic cooking. Shepherd's pie, chilli con carne, pastas with various sauces. She'd been so busy, there had hardly been time to think, but now the guilt came rushing in.

"You OK?" Andrew asked.

She gave him a shaky smile and said, "Last-minute jitters."

He put his hand over hers and gripped it firmly.

"I know," he said. "Bound to happen. But you've done the hard bit. The only thing left is to let go."

After a few minutes she said, "It's too late to go back, isn't it."

"I'm afraid so. Once the baggage is loaded, it causes a hell of an upset if anyone doesn't fly. They have to get all the bags off, chuck out the right one, reload, the plane misses its departure slot—"

"Don't," she said.

She released her hand from his grasp and sat back in her chair, struggling with her longing to be at home instead of looking out of these windows and waiting to go into the sky.

He watched her for a few moments, then said, "It may be just what they need, you know."

"Being alone together?" She gave a wry smile. "Dangerous."

"Nothing wrong with danger," said Andrew. "I've just been through the safest two years of my life, and it's driven me half insane. Not that I begrudge it – my mother had been very good to me. I owed her some time. But being so safe was tough."

He chuckled at the expression on Elaine's face.

"Don't worry. You're not running off with a maniac. I take my danger with due care. But I love these moments of standing at the edge of something new. Not knowing what lies ahead."

"I see what you mean," she said, because she was in the habit of agreeing.

But she didn't see, and her stomach was churning. She glanced across at the departure desk and saw the uniformed girl pick up her microphone.

"Flight number 324 to Rhodes is now ready for boarding through Gate Number One. Please have your passport and boarding pass ready for—"

"Right," said Andrew, getting to his feet. "Over the top. Don't fire till you see the whites of their eyes."

Elaine managed to laugh, but as she picked up her bag her head reeled. She seemed to be living in some extraordinary hallucination.

Part 2
Chapter 9

I'm sitting on the step of the bothy. She hasn't turned up yet, I don't know why. I sent her a text to say I'd be here at six, and it's well past that.

It's still hot and heavy and the sky is a dull grey colour. The birds aren't singing and there's no wind to move the leaves about, everything is waiting for the storm to break.

I don't know how long to hang on. She can't phone me, there's no signal here.

It's going to be harder to see her now, with both of us working. No more idle time to spend in private hours up the hill, exploring each other.

Yesterday she said, "It's like I've only ever been half of something. But now I'm with you it's like I'm complete, know what I mean? We're one thing."

It's like that for me, too. I only have to shut my eyes and I'm seeing her brown skin, her slim hands and feet, her strong-muscled legs, her white teeth. Feeling the strength and warmth of her.

Where *is* she?

The elderberry tree that sprawls across the bothy doorway has green berries on it. They won't be black until the autumn. Elaine picked a bucketful of them a few years back and made them into elderberry wine. McCasky tried it and said he didn't know why she bothered.

Big, heavy raindrops are plopping through the leaves. Damn. I hoped it would hold off until she got here. I get up from the step and go in. Lightning cracks across the sky and an explosion of thunder rolls on and on. Rain's coming down like someone's turned on the tap. It's battering on what's left of the roof and pouring in through the open bit where it's fallen in. The water's running out under the wall at the back, which is good. Half the floor is staying dry.

"Hi," she says from behind me. "Sorry I'm late. He made me do overtime."

Water's dripping off her. I wish I had a towel or something. She comes close and I run my hands down her back to try to dry her.

"Mmm, lovely," she says.

She turns her wet face up to mine.

Right now, I wouldn't care if this turned out to be the last moment of my life. I don't know what to do with all this happiness. It's like the day when I saw her on the boat but more, so much more, a huge power that's stronger than I am and a thousand times better.

She grabs my hair in her hands, pulling me close. Her skin is still wet, and the smell of her is wonderful. I kiss the hollow of her neck, and she wriggles a shoulder out of her rain-soaked shirt. Clothes are a nuisance, we're pushing them out of the way as best we can though they cling. Better. Oh, better. How beautiful she is. I kiss my way down to her warm breast and she gasps.

"Ah," she says. "Aaah."

Elaine sat cross-legged on her square blue mat. Seventeen other people sat likewise, listening earnestly. She wished she could lie down. The pursuit of tranquillity was proving to be quite energetic, and her back ached.

"Nothing new can come to you unless you make space for it," Alban said.

He was so lean and supple that his long legs folded easily into a perfect lotus position, flat to the floor. *Like a deck chair*, Elaine thought. His narrow hands rested palms up on his knees and his eyes were shut. His head wove to and fro a little as he spoke, like speeded-up film of a growing pea plant, probably because he was casting around so sensitively for new elements of the truth.

"We become too full," he said in his remote voice. "It is not our fault. From childhood, we are taught that we must get things and hold onto them. Knowledge. Relationships. Money." He smiled faintly as a piece of inspiration came. "We hoover these things up, and the point comes when we can hold no more. The motor begins to labour, the note rises to a high whine because it is stressed. So what do we do?"

Elaine, along with several other women, murmured, "Empty the bag."

"Yes, indeed," said Alban.

"Or the bin, if it is the bagless sort," put in a man called Gresham.

"You know you need to achieve emptiness," Alban went on as though Gresham had not spoken. "And yet you find it hard. All these things you have collected so carefully are valuable to you. So it is difficult to discard them."

Andrew was sitting on the far side of the room. He met Elaine's gaze for a moment then shifted back to a middle-distance stare. They would talk about this later.

Dolores, who was American, asked, "When you say 'things' – does that include people?"

"Yes," said Alban. "It has to."

He waited for a murmur of unease to peter out, then went on, "You will probably be thinking, *but they need me*. This will be true, for we all need each other – but be careful that you are not *needing* them to need you. Do not burden them. Let them be free."

"That's right," said Gresham eagerly. "Nobody wants to be jammed into someone else's vacuum bag. Or bin."

A couple of people rolled their eyes, but Dolores rose to the bait.

"If you really love someone, being jammed together is great," she said. "You want to share everything. Like it says in the Bible, 'Give and do not count the cost'. Isn't that right?"

"Giving is a beautiful thing," said Alban. "But if you give too much, it becomes a strain."

Rather firmly, he went on, "Before we break for our midday meal, we will have meditation. Do not strive for it. If you find thoughts arriving, gently let them go."

He picked up a pair of tiny temple bells linked by a red cord and touched them together. Their pure, high ting faded slowly into silence.

I'm no good at meditation, Elaine thought. It always made her wish she could sit on a chair instead of a mat.

Lunch break. I've left Bill reading *The Sun* and munching sandwiches untidily.

There's nothing much in the fridge. Two cold sausages from last night, so I scoff those. Raw vegetables in the drawers under the glass shelf. Useless. And the bread packet is empty.

There's a card beside it. Picture of two old women in black outside a church with geraniums at the window. I turn it over. And laugh. Most of it is taken up with instructions on how to use the washing machine. *Sorry*, she's written, *I forgot to put this on the list I left. Don't use the Boil setting except for dirty overalls*. Then stuff about woollens and sheets and the dial numbers. At the bottom she's put,

Do hope you are managing all right. The person I am replacing isn't back yet, so I might be here a bit longer. Much love. PS – I really do think about you. Elaine.

Huh. Better if she'd laid in some pizzas that we could microwave.

Hunt through the cupboards. Lentils, rice, dried beans of every possible sort, soy sauce. Herbal teas— Bingo. There's a munchy bar. Cereal with red fruits, that'll do.

There's no milk. I'll get a coffee from the machine in the office.

It's shadowy in here, but the stone walls are still warm. We're sitting on an old log I brought in. Kerry is leaning against me and my arm is round her. I ought to be feeling OK, but I'm not really. Apart from anything else, I'm very hungry. I'll scrounge something from the kitchen when I get back. McCasky should be settled in front of the TV by then. He's been very ratty since Elaine went.

"Cal, if you could live anywhere you wanted," Kerry says, "where would you choose?"

I've never thought about it.

"Dunno. Lots of places."

"Yes, but after you've been round the world and seen everything. Where would you be really happy?"

I remember looking down from the plane at a city spread like a rash on the world's skin.

"A tent," I say.

"In the winter?"

"Um. Got a point."

There was a poem Elaine used to say to us when we were kids, something about Innisfree. *A small cabin build there, of clay and wattles made.* She said a cabin meant a hut.

"Could go for a hut."

"This is a kind of hut," she says. "You'd only have to clean it out and mend the roof, and you could live in it."

So that's what she was leading up to. But I don't mind. I've thought the same.

"You mean, we could live in it."

"If you wanted to."

She's looking at me, frowning a bit.

"Cal," she says. "You do mean it, don't you?"

"About living here?"

"Not just that. I mean, you won't go away or anything?"

Her black eyes are searching mine, she really wants an answer. I don't know why she has to ask.

"Don't be daft. 'Course I won't."

"You might think this is just – one of those summer things. You know?"

She's trying to smile, but it's not working very well. Why is she so anxious? I turn to look at her.

"I couldn't be without you," I tell her. "It would be like – I don't know. Like trying to live without my brain or something."

"Are you sure?"

"Of course I'm sure. And if I go anywhere else, you'll have to come too."

"Oh, good."

But she's still frowning a bit.

I wish we were older. I wish I had money, so I could look after her.

Hang on. I can't have had that thought. Money is what's mucking up the world.

Kerry leans her folded arms on her knees, staring at the floor.

"You'll think I'm being stupid, going on about all this," she says. "It's not like I want to be dependent on you or anything. I'll work. It's just I want to know you'll be there."

There's a bit of a silence, then she says, "There's something I've got to tell you."

"Go on."

"Well there was someone in Australia."

So Jess was right.

"I was only fourteen, it was stupid. But he was dead good-looking and really nice, he made me feel kinda … safe. Derek kicked up hell when he found out."

She always calls her father Derek, same as I think of mine as McCasky. I don't call him that, though. I don't really call him anything.

"But see," Kerry's saying, "Derek's not my real father. He's just my mum's husband."

"You're joking."

"I'm *not* joking. *Look* at me." She holds out her brown arms. "I'm not some white Pom's kid, am I? Get real."

"Sorry. But I mean—"

"My father was a Koori."

She used that word before, about a museum, but I don't understand it.

"What's a Koori?"

"An Aborigine. A native Australian. One of the people who were there before the Whitefellas came and murdered them and took their land. He was in charge of the Museum of Aboriginal Life near where Mum and Derek lived. Mum told me about it. She said she felt privileged that he liked her."

It all drops into place.

"So that's how you know about Aboriginal music."

"Yeah. Mum used to take me to corroborees at the museum. Kind of concerts, only not for public entertainment. People singing and dancing, telling the old stories."

"Like a ceilidh."

"Yeah, kinda. I wish I knew more about Koori music. It's hard to find out, because I don't belong with them. Don't belong anywhere, really."

I'm trying to think through what happened.

"Your mum and the guy at the museum – did she feel about him like…"

I was going to say, *like I do about you*, but I don't have to.

"Yes, she did. She told me. But she'd not long been

116

married to Derek, and he adored her. They'd been trying for a baby, so he was dead pleased when she got pregnant. Mum had all her fingers crossed that I'd be white. She couldn't be sure, you see. She hoped Derek was the father. But when I was born, they knew he wasn't."

I put my hand over my face. I can imagine what he'd have said.

Kerry's still talking. "My proper name's Rebecca. But Derek always called me the Koori. Mum said when I started to talk I said that, too. It sounded like Kerry. So it stuck."

"It's a great name. Better than Rebecca."

She doesn't stop.

"They had my brothers afterwards, Neil then Micky. Proper white boys. That's fine. I love them and all that, I really do. And – I guess I'm useful."

I remembered her on the boat, dealing with the younger one's tantrum, holding him up at the window, showing him the island. Yes, dead useful.

"Have you ever met your real father?"

She shakes her head.

"He went away. Kooris are like that. It drives white Australians mad, 'specially the teachers. The Koori kids at school seem all settled in, then suddenly they've gone walkabout and nobody knows where. Mum says it's because there are things more important to them."

We're quiet for a bit, thinking about it.

"See," she says, "you're kind of – proper."

I'm outraged.

"I'm *not* proper!"

"Don't get me wrong, you're crazy same as me, but at least you've got a dad who really is your dad. I fancied you right from the start but I thought, nah, he's just a shy boy from a nice family. When I heard you play I knew you were different. But I still tried to keep off."

"I noticed."

"Yeah. I'm sorry about that. It was partly because of Derek. After the guy in Australia, he watches me like a hawk. So I tried to be careful. But after I got to know you I just – stopped trying."

"I'm glad," I say.

And she cuddles up and sighs happily.

"Me, too."

Chapter 10

It's late when I get back, but the lights are on and there's music coming from the house. That's weird. It's not the TV. It's Ry Cooder.

I go in through the conservatory and pause at the door of the living room. McCasky says, "Is that you, Cal? Come on in."

He's sitting on the big sofa beside a blonde woman in white trousers and a flowered sleeveless top. She's very suntanned. He finds the remote and cuts the volume a bit then says, "Do you know Kitty Reed? Kitty, this is my son Callum."

"Hi," she says. "Great to meet you."

I suppose I ought to go and shake hands or something, but I'm too gobsmacked.

Kitty Reed shifts her glass to the other hand and pats the seat beside her.

"Come in and join the party."

There are Pringles on the table beside various bottles and cans, and olives in a dish. He's been shopping, hasn't he. Unless Kitty brought them.

"And how's your evening been?" he asks.

By which he means, *Some of us see our girlfriends in comfort, not in some midgy place up the hill*.

"Fine," I say.

More than fine, but it's none of his business.

I advance within grabbing reach and stuff some Pringles into my mouth. I'm too hungry to have any pride.

"I did chicken breasts in bacon," Kitty says, "with a wine sauce. If you're hungry, there's plenty left. It's in the kitchen. There's Black Forest gateau in the fridge. I didn't make that, though, it's Co-op."

I don't care what she's doing here, the woman is fabulous.

"You two haven't met, have you?" McCasky says. "I built Kitty's swimming pool."

"Yeah. Great."

Chicken. And gateau. This is no time for idle conversation.

"I'll – um – see you in a minute."

I bolt for the kitchen. I can hear them laughing, but I don't care.

I pick up a lump of chicken, discard the toothpick that's holding the bacon in place and bite into it. Marvellous. Cold roast potatoes, too.

I eat the lot, even the French beans. I'm leaning against the sink, spooning in gateau, when McCasky comes in.

"All right?" he says.

"Mmm."

Can't talk, got a mouthful.

"Kitty's going to stay for a few days. Help out while your mother's away. Do the shopping, keep the place tidy. Just so you know she'll be around."

"Oh. Right."

"When you've got a problem you have to find a solution," he says.

I suppose it's some sort of excuse.

"Sure," I say.

There's a moment while it looks as if he might offer something else, but it doesn't happen. He just says, "Stick the kettle on when you've finished. We'll have some coffee."

"OK."

He goes back to the sitting room. Ry Cooder has ended. He puts a new CD on. Dolly bloody Parton.

Jess is back from Kuala Lumpur. We're sprawled on my bed like she was never away. But everything's different. She's horrified about Kitty.

"I've only been away a couple of weeks, and I come back to find some floozy in the kitchen shelling peas. What on earth does he think he's doing? What's going to happen when Elaine comes back? And when *is* she coming back?

That postcard is just plain ridiculous. Honestly, our parents are such lunatics."

"Well, yes."

I wish Kerry had heard that. We're not so proper as she thinks.

"How's Kerry?" Jess asks, as if she can see into my head. She's always been good at that.

"She's fine," I say.

Jess looks at me. She takes a breath as if she's going to say something difficult.

"Cal. This is a dead personal question, and you can tell me to shut up if you like, but – are you and her having it off?"

My face has turned scarlet. It's nothing to do with her.

"OK," Jess says, getting the message, "why don't I get lost. But – you remember when I had a thing going with Mark."

"'Course."

How could I forget? McCasky was raging and Elaine was going around looking like a worried ghost.

"I thought I was pregnant," Jess says. "It scared me to death. Mark, too. Turned out to be a false alarm, but I'll never forget it."

"You never said." I feel a bit miffed.

"You were only eleven."

"Twelve."

"Were you? Well, doesn't matter. What I'm saying is,

at least Mark used a condom. He wasn't very good at it, but if I *had* been pregnant, I'd have had some excuse. Not my fault if the condom failed. But you wouldn't have any excuse. Right?"

I shake my head. I don't want to be having this conversation. I wish she'd shut up. Go away. Get lost.

Jess reaches down to the floor for her bag and fishes around in it.

"Here."

She puts a packet into my hand. Oh, my God. *Cherry flavoured*. I shove it quickly into the drawer of my bedside table and say, "Thanks," as if it's nothing at all. My hair's all over my face, so I don't have to look at her.

"I know how you feel," Jess says. "It makes you want to run away and hide. The thing is to try using one while you're on your own. That way, you get to know what you're doing. Think of it as – installing software."

She grins. OK, I get it. Soft-wear.

I aim a thump in her direction, but I have to laugh.

"C'mon," she says, then thinks of something else funny. "It's not exactly rocket science."

Rocket. Jet-propelled. But I wonder—

"Jess – do you carry them all the time?"

"Yeah, of course. Be Prepared, like every Girl Guide knows. Be a shame to turn down a nice opportunity because you're not equipped."

I thump my head.

"And I thought you just hung around with Mairi."

"Kid," she says in an American accent, "you don't know nothin' yet."

Perhaps she's right.

Elaine laid her ice-cream spoon in the saucer beside the tall glass. If anything, eating all that cold, sweet stuff had made her feel even hotter. They were sitting under the canopy's shade outside the cafe by the harbour, and the sun sparkled on the water and the unmoving boats. The orange fishing nets hanging up to dry were the colour of Callum's hair.

Sweat trickled down her back. Alban didn't hold classes in the afternoons – it was a time for "private realization", as he called it. The more gung-ho students went off to explore monasteries or swim, but Elaine was already uncomfortably sun-scorched in spite of high-factor cream and more sun was not a good idea.

Worry lurked just below the surface. She'd given in after only a small argument when Andrew suggested they should stay a bit longer, but after sending the postcard, she'd kept wondering if Callum was all right. She ought to have enabled her phone for overseas roaming before she left, but she hadn't known about that. Andrew said she could use his, but that meant if Cal called back he'd get Andrew instead of her. Not to speak of the danger that Fergus might spot the number. She felt queasy at the thought.

"Alban's right about making space," Andrew remarked.

"Yes. But how are you supposed to do it?"

She knew she sounded peevish and ungrateful, but she couldn't help it. She pushed a strand of hair back from her face. It felt limp and sweaty between her fingers, like a dying plant stem. Andrew was watching her.

"Why don't you get your hair cut short?" he suggested. "It would be cooler for you."

"Heavens. Do you think I could?"

She hadn't considered changing it for years. She'd always thought women who fussed about their hair were frivolous. And tying it back was so easy.

"Why not?" said Andrew. "It might be the sort of space-making that Alban means. Cast off assumptions."

"And hair."

She laughed, suddenly excited. There was a little hair-dresser's in a back street near the market square, with old pictures of film stars in the window, faded to pale greenish-blue. Nobody in such a shop would start persuading her into smart styling or coloured rinses. It would just be a simple trim. Nothing fancy.

He glanced at his watch. "Nearly four. The shops will be opening again. Let's go and see what we can find."

I've been running the store on my own this morning. McCasky said to phone the office if there were any problems, but I didn't have to. I managed the card machine and everything. Bill had to go to the dentist. He called the office first thing to say he was in agony. I hope he comes back soon, I'm ravenous, but I can't leave the store unattended.

A man comes in wanting paving slabs. They're outside with the sand and gravel and stuff.

I go out and help him load thirty slabs into his van. We come back in for him to pay for them. Bill's turned up. He's over there talking to some bloke about paintbrushes.

When I've put the card through the machine for the paving slabs Bill comes to ring up cash for three brushes. He's a good salesman.

When the customer's gone I ask, "You OK?"

He looks a bit pale and one side of his face is swollen.

"Fine," he says. "He did a lovely job. Never felt a thing."

"Did he take it out, then?"

"Had to. I'd an abcess."

A woman comes in for an extension lead. She says she cut hers in half with the Flymo and fused everything.

"I'll get it," I say to Bill. "You sit down."

She doesn't know how long the lead needs to be so I have to talk, ask her how big her garden is. Tennis court size? Half a tennis court? When we've settled what she wants and she's paid, Bill is still sitting down.

He says, "Time for new ones."

I'm still thinking about extension leads, so I say, "New what?"

"Teeth. He said some of them will last a bit yet—"

"That's good," I say, but he doesn't agree.

"Nah. Have the lot out and be done with it. I had bad teeth when I was a kid, and every time my mum took me to the dentist it hurt like buggery. So when I grew up I didn't go."

I'm not surprised. Poor bloke.

It seems a bit tactless to talk about eating, but I really am hungry.

"I'll just go over to the house and grab a sandwich," I say. "I'll be right back. Can I get you anything?"

"Wouldn't mind a cup of tea," says Bill.

He's not the complaining sort.

Kitty's left a note on the table that says, *Cornish pasty in microwave, strawberries and yogurt in the fridge.*

I press the microwave button. The light goes on and the pasty starts going round.

Elaine hasn't been in touch since that one postcard. It's over three weeks now. I'm starting to wonder if she'll ever come back. McCasky hasn't said anything about it, and I can't ask him. I sort of miss her, but not as much as I ought to. I mean, she's my mother and everything, but with Kitty here, it's so easy.

She's never around at lunchtime but there's always stuff in the fridge and the microwave, or else a good pile of sandwiches. She does the washing, too. She stuck a note on my door that said, *Anything in the washing basket gets washed. Nothing else.* So I hauled out a lot of stinky old stuff that was lying around on my floor and bunged it in the basket and right enough, it got done.

I don't know about her and McCasky. She makes him laugh, which is pretty amazing. In fact, he's going round looking dead pleased with himself. He hasn't said anything about the situation since that night when he told me she'd be staying for a few days, but I guess they're both enjoying themselves. From my point of view, it's got to be good.

Maybe that's how it works. One queen ant moves out, another one moves in. I'm just a mindless worker, I don't have any choice. McCasky and I fit in because she provides what we need. In our different ways. According to our status.

The microwave pings. I open the door and the smell of hot Cornish pasty comes wafting out. Sit down at the table with it, start noshing.

Ants aren't like us, though. They don't do sex. Only the queens, if they survive that first flight when most of them don't make it. The rest just do the job they're meant for. Our government would go for that. No demonstrations, no argument. It would save them a lot of problems if they microchipped every kid at birth so it grew up to be a sexless worker. A few could be drones who have it off with a princess if they're lucky, then get dumped.

That would be me. One shot, then off to be recycled into fertilizer or something. Not sitting here, eating strawberries after demolishing a Cornish pasty. Not getting up to make an instant milkshake. Good idea of Kitty's, that. I like the green one, it's excellently disgusting. Kind of Gothic milkshake made of lime-flavoured cave-slime. If you don't die of misery, life has its fun moments.

I'll make a thermos of tea for Bill. Some dentist is in for an interesting time with him. In a weird kind of way, I'm fascinated.

McCasky comes into the store a bit before closing time.

"Bill's gone home," I tell him. "He said to tell you he'd make the time up."

McCasky nods. "You've done well today," he says. "Earned yourself a bonus."

"Thanks."

"School starts before long," he goes on. "What do you plan to do? We're assuming you want to go back, but is that right?"

I don't have a plan. I want to live with Kerry in the bothy. McCasky demolished an old caravan last week and bunged all the stuff from it into the scrap store, so we've got a yellow plastic water carrier with a lid now, and a camping gas stove. And mugs and spoons. But the summer won't go on much longer. We're into August, and the daylight is getting shorter.

I shrug. "Got to go back, I suppose."

"And do what?"

Can't answer. Don't know.

"Look, Cal, I can't afford to have you idling about the place," he goes on. "You've got two choices. You either go back to school and put the work in, with some idea of what you do at the end of it, or you stay on here as a full-time apprentice."

I don't want to look at him, but my hair's tied back, there's no curtain. He scares me. He's always scared me. When I was a little kid, he used to pick me up and chuck me in the air and I'd scream because I wasn't sure he'd catch me. He'd laugh. I think he thought I was enjoying it.

"Fuck's sake," he says, "it's not a bad option. Parents ask me all the time if I'll take their kids on. You can do day release for college. And you've a big advantage. There's a business to step into if you want it. One of these days."

I know he'd like that. His father left it to him, he leaves it to me. But I don't want it. Juggling all that money, building houses then wondering if anyone will buy them, employing people who'll depend on me for wages. Whatever I do, it's got to be on my own. So I can live with Kerry and not get involved in anything else.

"Well?" he says.

"I'll go back to school."

"And?"

"Work."

"All right. Chosen your subjects for Highers?"

"Music."

"What else?"

"Biology."

Because of the ants. There's a lot more I'd like to know.

"And Technology, perhaps."

Jess would laugh, after what I said about her horrible robots. I wouldn't go for cybernetics though. Earth sciences could be more use.

"All right," McCasky says, and holds out his large, dirty hand. "That a deal?"

"Yes."

We shake on it. There's no way I can make my grip as tough as his, and he's not even trying.

"I'll lock up here," he says. "Go and meet your girl."

But there's a text from Kerry to say she can't come. Her parents are going to a meal with the guy who runs Island Paragliding so she's lumbered with baby-sitting.

Kitty's done steak and kidney pie. We're sitting round the table in the conservatory, with proper serving dishes and stuff.

McCasky's phone rings.

"McCasky Groundworks."

He lifts another forkful, then stops.

"Well, well," he says. "So what's been happening – or shouldn't I ask?"

Kitty picks up her plate and goes into the kitchen.

It's got to be Elaine. I'm pretending I don't know.

McCasky listens while he goes on eating one-handed.

"So you've made up your mind," he says.

He pushes his chair back from the table and goes out into the garden. I watch him while I eat some more pie and another spud. He's sitting at the picnic table with his back to me.

When he comes back in he says, "That was your mother. From Glasgow."

"Is she coming home?"

"Bit of a maybe."

"Why?"

He gives me a considering look, then makes up his mind.

"You may as well know. She's found herself another man."

Chapter 11

"*Wow,*" Kerry says. "So what's going to happen? Where's she going to live?"

"I don't know."

There's still a bit of daylight in the sky outside but it's dark in here. I got a gas lamp from the scrap store, though, and bought a new cylinder. It makes a pool of light round where we're sitting. I made this table and bench, too.

She goes on, "But you'll need to know, won't you?"

"Jess will find out. I phoned her this afternoon. She's back in Glasgow, earning some money before she starts at uni. She says she'll talk to Elaine."

"Why do you always call her Elaine?"

"Dunno, really. I always have. Jess, too, we both did. I suppose it's what she wanted. When I started primary school I tried calling her Mum like the other kids called their mothers, but she said it was like calling a cat 'Cat'."

"Why don't you phone her yourself?"

Scary. I wouldn't know where to start.

"Jess does that kind of thing. Girl stuff."

"*What?* You prejudiced old git!"

"Don't be stupid."

"I am *not stupid*."

I hate it when she gets into these bad moods. She's been really nippy lately.

"Sorry," I say. "But I'm not prejudiced. You know I'm not."

"Do I? You might be anything. You've got these big ideas, but none of it's real. OK, I love you and everything, but sometimes I wish…"

She looks away as if there's no point in trying to tell me.

"Wish *what?*"

"Never mind."

"I *do* mind. I want to know."

She turns back to face me.

"All right, then. I wish you'd just *grow* up."

"Fuck's sake."

I sound like McCasky, but I don't care. This is so unfair. Why can't she understand?

"I've been doing my best to make this place decent, I've lugged stuff up here from the store, earned the money to pay for it, I built this table and bench and—"

"Yeah, OK, OK. What about *us?*"

"Everything I do is for us. I never think about anything else."

"Yes, you do. You think about how great it is to have

a girlfriend and play at having adventures. It's like Enid bloody Blyton. It's not real."

"Like, working in the store isn't real? I've been running the place on my own today because Bill—"

"Oh, big deal."

She looks away, arms folded.

This is awful. We've never had a row.

"Kerry – please…"

She sighs.

"Guess it's my fault too. I just got carried away, never mind about being careful."

Careful.

Oh. Is *that* what she means? If so, then it's trump card time. I fish out the packet Jess gave me. Like she said, it was difficult trying it out but I'm glad I did. I only got round to it three nights ago, but I feel good about it now.

"I've been thinking about being careful. Look."

Kerry looks. And she laughs, sort of.

"Now he tells me," she says.

She puts the back of her hand over her mouth and shuts her eyes. I think she's trying not to cry. This is awful.

"Kerry, what is it?"

I put my arm round her. The breath goes out of her and she rests against me like she's very tired.

"What is it?" I ask again. "You've got to tell me."

She gives a long sigh. "Taking care," she says. "You're too late. I'm pregnant."

The moment goes on and on. Everything tumbles into pieces.

"How long have you known?"

"Not long. I've just missed once. But I feel sick and everything. I'm sure."

She looks up, suddenly fierce. "And before you say anything, you've got to know, I'm not getting rid of it. So if that idea's going through your head, you can forget it. My mum could have got rid of me, and been on the safe side. But she didn't. And if she could do that for her kid, I can do it for mine."

Oh, my God.

I'm thinking back frantically. It must have been that first time, on the night of the thunderstorm. Or afterwards, I suppose. Several times afterwards.

"I can't tell my parents," she says. "Derek will be furious."

So will McCasky. I've been so stupid. How can something so awesome happen just because you simply love someone? But I suppose that's what love is for. It's got its own purpose. It uses you to make more people. Like Kerry says, it's not Enid Blyton.

"That's why I asked if you'd stick around," she says. "But now you know – I guess you won't."

I don't stop to think. "Yes, I will."

But it's true.

"Go on?"

She looks at me in real surprise. All this time, she's been facing up to being on her own. No wonder she was ratty sometimes.

"Are you sure?" she asks. "I mean, you don't like people. And we're going to make another one."

"Yes, but – oh, shit."

She's right. I've added to the humans. I can't just live as if I'm programmed, there's no queen ant to take charge, I'm on my own. If anyone's in charge, it's me. And I've blown it.

Why don't I mind more? I'm dead scared. Totally clobbered. I've wrecked everything and McCasky is going to kill me and yet underneath it all there's a weird excitement. What the hell is that about?

Kerry's watching me.

"I knew you wouldn't like it," she says.

"It's not a question of liking."

"So what is it?"

"Just – I've got to get my head round it."

Try to find something that's OK. And there's only one thing.

"Ours will be different. It won't add to—" I'm finding this hard to say. "To all the – the mess."

And suddenly it comes together, the years of feeling guilty that I'm stuck with being a human, the wreckage of the world, the pointlessness of school, McCasky scaring me shitless, all the fury and misery. And the oh-so-careful conversations with Pirelli and people looking at me sideways because they know I'm a nutter. They're right, I am. But it's all I've got, that's what I am. Tears come, and I scrub furiously at my eyes with the back of my wrist.

"Oh, Cal. I'm sorry. Look, you needn't worry. I'll be all right. You don't have to—"

"Yes, I do." I push my hair back so I can look at her properly. "Kerry – humans don't have to be hellish. I thought they all were, but you're different. We've made – we're going to make – someone who's OK."

It sounds like rubbish. But she puts her hands on either side of my face and looks at me, and there are tears in her eyes, too.

"Yes," she says. "Please, God. Yes, we will."

There was nothing outside the hotel window except a white-tiled wall about six metres away. Elaine drew the curtains and sat down on the bed. Andrew was in the shower.

They won't have touched the garden, she thought. *The runner beans will be going to waste. Courgettes rotting on the ground. Slugs eating the lettuce.*

In the white walls and blue sky of the Greek island, she'd been too far from the garden to think about it, but the sharp air of Scotland brought back the desire to pull weeds out of damp soil and smell the green sweetness of tomato plants. *Oh, my tomato plants. They'll be a wreckage.*

How illogical was that? She should be thinking about

her husband and her children, not tomato plants.

Her phone rang, startling her. Of course – they were back in Britain so it worked again. She fished it out of her handbag and said, "Hello?"

"Elaine – it's Jess."

"Oh, darling, how lovely to hear you. How was Malaysia, did you have a good time?"

"Fine. Pop phoned."

"Oh."

"Where are you?"

"In a hotel in Glasgow." Andrew had suggested going to the house in Kilmarnock, but she wanted to get home. We're coming to the island tomorrow morning."

"We?"

"Me and Andrew."

There was a short pause, then Jess said, "Is he there with you now?'

"He's in the shower."

"Not the best time to talk, then."

"It depends on what you want to say," Elaine said.

"Well – there's quite a lot, isn't there? Like, are you going to live on the island? Like, will we see you again? Or are you shoving off forever – to bloody Kilmarnock?"

Her voice held its usual toughness, but it wobbled on the last words. She was quickly back in control, though.

"Sorry. I don't want to lay a heavy emotional number on you. Just – there's a lot of stuff to sort out."

"Yes, there is. Darling, I do know how upsetting this must be."

"Well," Jess said, "you've a right to lead your own life. If you've been unhappy, I wouldn't want it to go on like that. I knew things were a bit iffy between you and Pop, but—"

"How's he been?" asked Elaine.

"Fine. More than fine. In fact, I might as well tell you, because you'll need to know at some point. He's been seeing Kitty Reed. Know who I mean? The swimming pool woman. She's practically moved in."

"Oh, my goodness. When you say *in*, you mean…?"

"I mean she does the shopping and cooking and the laundry. Cleans the house, looks after the garden…"

She left it for Elaine to put the big question.

"And stays the night?"

"Yes. Sorry, but yes."

"I see."

Andrew came out of the shower with a towel round his middle, and foraged in his case for a clean shirt. He cocked an eyebrow at her and she mouthed, "Jess". He nodded and dropped a kiss on the top of her head, and Elaine missed what Jess was saying.

"Sorry, darling, I was distracted for a moment. Say again?"

"Never mind," said Jess. "I'll call you later. Bye."

And she'd gone.

* * *

Lunch break. Note from Kitty as usual, so McCasky can't have told her about Elaine. Or perhaps he has, and she's doing a few last things.

Chicken pie in microwave. Yogurts.

Click the button, light goes on.

It's really busy in the store. Bill has taken a few days off. He's having his teeth out, all the rest of them. Horrendous, but I suppose he knows what he wants. McCasky's got an old bloke in to help mind the store, Charlie Angus, but he's slow and he can't get the hang of the card machine.

I wish I knew what's going to happen. Jess said Elaine and her bloke would be back on the island today, but I don't suppose she'll come here. I keep feeling kind of upset, but like Kerry said, I need to grow up. One thing's for sure, I can't tell anyone about the baby. 'Specially not Jess. She'll start banging on about how Kerry should get an abortion right now, before it goes any further. But it's not her business. It's nothing to do with anyone, just Kerry and me.

Everyone's going to know, though. It'll start to show. Don't know when — by about Christmas I suppose. Maybe sooner. I feel queasy at the thought. Kerry feels sick all the time, she says.

The microwave pings. I put the pie on a plate. I'm hungry but the birdy-oily smell of it is off-putting. Could be better in the garden, it's hot and stuffy in here.

I go up the path to the flat bit at the top where there are a couple of white plastic garden chairs.

I don't know if Kerry and I can go back to school. Might be difficult for her. It's OK for me, I suppose. I'd been thinking I'd get stuck in this year and maybe go for dentistry after all. I know what Miss Irvine said, and she's right. But I'll need to earn money. And if we have to have people, it's better if they're not in pain and talking with their mouths half shut because they don't want anyone to see their grotty teeth. Not that Bill ever bothered, you got treated to a grin that was more black than white, like it was quite normal. Wonder how he's got on.

The ants are swarming. It's a hot, still day, and they're boiling up through cracks between stones and out of little holes, fussing round big, winged ones that look a bit clumsy and hapless. They'll be young queens. Most of them won't get anywhere. Built-in wastage.

I eat a bit of the pie but I can't cope with it. I dump it on the ground. The ants don't take any notice. They're in Flying Day mode, so food's not on the agenda. Clouds of the new ones are rising into the air. Most of them are hopeless, but there are a few stronger ones that look halfway capable. The wastage is colossal, but that's the way the design works. Put them all to the test, wait for a single hero to win through and mate with the young queen. Like that song in the *Snow White* film, "Some Day My Prince Will Come". The workers don't care about the crawling crash-landers, they just go on chivvying the ones that haven't taken off yet. The wings are falling off the failed fliers. There's getting to be a scatter of these little transparent wings all over the ground, like discarded cherry petals. Confetti after a wedding. Only ants don't have weddings, they just do what they have to.

All those wings. All that time to create something so perfect and throw it away. But I guess that's the way it is. Make a lot, pick the best, blow the rest.

Scary.

Chapter 12

Elaine sat on a leather sofa in the smaller, less public lounge of the Marina Hotel in Colbeag, waiting for Fergus. He was only five minutes late so far, but it was starting to seem like a long time. A waiter had asked if she'd like something, and she'd ordered a bottle of still water. She didn't approve of bottled water – all that plastic, and the transport cost – but she'd chickened out of saying tap water would do.

Fergus walked past without seeing her as he headed towards the bigger lounge, then did a double-take and came back. He was in grubby jeans and a checked shirt with the sleeves rolled up.

"Didn't recognize you for a moment," he said. "Like the new hairstyle."

The Greek hairdresser had been charming, and surprisingly sophisticated. He'd talked her into a short, ash-blonde bob.

Fergus sat down beside her. "Sorry to be late," he went on. "Stupid boy turned round with a running chainsaw, made a mess of his leg."

She gasped. "Not Cal?"

"No, not Cal. Angus Finnie. Nineteen, old enough to know better. Ambulance case, accident report, all that stuff."

A waiter appeared and he ordered a beer. Elaine said she was all right with the water.

"So," Fergus said. "Where have you been?"

"In Greece, like I said."

"But not working."

"No."

"So who's this man?"

"Andrew Duncan."

"Is he from the island?"

"No. He was looking after his mother on the mainland, in her house in Kilmarnock. She had cancer. Then she died. It's his house now. He doesn't have anywhere else, he's been abroad a lot. He came over here to stay with his sister for a bit. Patsy Carradine."

Fergus nodded, digesting this.

"So what's the plan?" he asked.

"He wants – I mean, we want to live together."

Her change of wording didn't escape him. "Was this his idea or yours?"

I mustn't put the blame on Andrew. That's cowardice.

"It wasn't just him." She took a deep breath. "I know I need to explain, but it's difficult. He's so – *kind*."

"Easy to be kind if you've plenty of money."

"That's not fair. Some people just *are* kind—"

"And others aren't."

I've done it wrong again. Take a deep breath.

"Fergus, I do feel terrible about this."

"But not terrible enough."

The waiter came with the beer. Fergus drank half of it. Elaine seized the chance of a small counter-attack.

"Jess phoned last night. She said you've found someone else."

"I *needed* someone else," he said. "You left me in a hole. I can't take time off work to stand in a queue at the Co-op, and the place was getting to be a tip. So I asked Kitty Reed to help out."

"It was more than that, though."

He was unfazed.

"So?"

I'm not jealous, Elaine thought. *I'm in no position to be jealous. But...*

"Is she going to be permanent?"

Fergus shrugged.

"Her husband works in Saudi. He's back on leave shortly."

"I see."

Oh, dear. I sound like some tight-lipped headmistress.

"Look, Elaine, face facts. Yes, I moved Kitty in. I slept

with her. But you're here to tell me you're leaving, right? Going to live with Andrew in Kilmarnock or wherever."

Her face flamed, infuriatingly.

"Well – yes."

He finished his beer and leaned back against the leather sofa, looking at her. Then he laughed.

"I never thought you had it in you," he said.

He held out his hand, and after a moment she took it.

"If you fancy this guy, I can live with that," he said. "So why don't you come back? Cal needs a mother, he's young yet. Look after your garden, do your therapy if it matters that much. Go on seeing Andrew if you want. Get him to buy a place here if he's awash with money."

For a dizzying moment it sounded perfect, but of course it wasn't. Andrew was a man who made his own decisions – she'd never suggested anything to him, just said yes or no.

Fergus was watching her.

"C'mon, hen," he said with a return to the Scots that seldom surfaced through his neutral working-man voice. "It's no' the end of the world."

He returned her hand to her own knee and gave it a firm pat.

"Got to go," he said. "Give me a call when you've made up your mind."

Then he went out, pulling his wallet from his pocket and waving at the waiter.

* * *

Another lunchtime. It won't be chicken pie. Won't be anything now Kitty's left. I come out of the store and cross the yard to the house. There's a women in the garden, weeding. Short blonde hair. Not Kitty, she's more goldy-colour. This one is paler – sort of primrose-white.

Jeez. It's Elaine.

I start up the steps towards her. She looks up and sees me. Drops her handful of weeds and comes hurrying down, all flustered.

"There's pizza—" she starts to say, but I've reached her and she's hugging me and I'm hugging her back. She seems smaller, somehow.

"Are you all right?" she says.

"Yeah, fine. I've been working in the store."

"I know. Your dad said."

"You've met him?"

"Yes. We had a talk. It was all very civilized. Would you rather eat in the conservatory or the kitchen?"

"Kitchen's fine."

She takes a pizza from the oven, not the microwave. It's home-made. Salami and olives.

When she's served it out and added some salad to hers she says, "Are you still seeing Kerry?"

I've got a mouthful so I just nod. The secret fills the kitchen and makes me feel breathless.

You're not to tell anyone, Kerry said. *Derek mustn't know until it's too late for him to make me get rid of it.*

We just eat for a bit. I don't know what to say about Greece. It's not the kind of situation where you ask to see the holiday snaps.

"Oh, there's a letter," she remembers.

She takes it from beside the bread bin and passes it across. I tear it open, still munching. It's from the Health people. They don't say anything about Pirelli leaving to get married, just that a new session of consultations is due to begin next week. Perhaps he's changed his mind and he'll be there after all. I push it across the table to Elaine, and she gets her glasses out to read it. Then she looks up.

"Has it been any use?"

"Dunno, really."

It hasn't made me feel newly wise and happy, if that's what she's hoping. But at least he's harmless.

"I quite like him."

"You may as well go on, then," Elaine says.

"Could do."

Jess has found a flat in Govan. I could stay overnight. Take Kerry with me, perhaps. Jess doesn't know yet, but she'll be all right about it. She's the one person I can trust.

When we've finished the pizza, Elaine gets a lemon meringue pie out of the fridge.

"Wow," I say. "I'm really glad you're back!"

It's meant as a joke, but my mother has never been much good at knowing when I'm joking.

"Are you?" she says. "That's nice." But she's looking bothered again.

"Cal, things aren't quite settled yet."

"Oh."

Bit of a downer.

"I thought you were back."

She folds her arms on the table while I eat. She isn't into lemon meringue pie.

"You know I have this friend, of course. Andrew. He's a nice person. Very kind and understanding. I think you'd like him."

I go on eating.

Elaine tries again. "This is only an idea, but – it may be we can all respect each other. Not be too selfish about it."

She's hoping I'll say something, but I can't. I'm beginning to go off the sharp taste of the pie. I've propped the side of my head on my hand, spooning in very small bits.

"We might be able to come to a civilized arrangement," she says. "If Andrew was based here – or even if we saw him in Kilmarnock sometimes…"

No. She can't mean it. But she does.

"I just wondered if – well – if we could all get on. Share our lives."

I nearly choke. I don't want to get on with some tosser who shagged my mother.

"He'd love to get to know you," she says.

I finish the last of the pie, and sit with my hands in my

lap, staring at the spoon and the yellow-smeared plate. I feel slightly sick. And what about McCasky? Living with him is like cuddling up to a time bomb, but he's been better since I started working in the store.

Elaine guesses what I'm thinking – not that it's difficult.

"Your dad and I had a very reasonable talk," she says. "You see, Cal – grown-up people sometimes have to find different patterns for their lives."

"I know."

I almost laugh. She doesn't know how much I know. Me and Kerry – we're a time bomb, too. I'm not just a kid who's being asked to share two dads. Find a different pattern? Well, yeah. And how. I push my chair back and stand up.

"Better get back."

She looks disappointed. "That's a short lunch break," she says.

"Things are busy in the store," I say. I sound like McCasky.

"Yes. I expect they are." She's heard that too often.

I give her a quick kiss and say, "See you later."

But I don't know if I will.

I set off across the yard.

Things are more of a mess than ever.

"Hi, Cal" says Pirelli. "Had a good summer?"

"Yeah, OK."

"Been away?"

"No. Working for my father."

"Interesting job?"

"Not bad. He's a builder. I've been helping in the store."

"What about school? You were wondering whether to do another year."

"I've said I'll go back."

I'm frowning. I don't know if I can tell him about Kerry. On the boat I decided I would, but it's not that easy. It's got to be now if I do it at all, though. This is the last session before he hands over to the Janet woman. He's just explained that.

He's still waiting.

"Thing is, something's happened."

"A change for the better?"

He's trying to be helpful but I can't look at him, my hair is all over my face. Nothing for it. I blurt the words out.

"Kerry's going to have a baby."

He's perfectly calm.

"Have you told anyone else?"

"No. Kerry made me promise I wouldn't. She's scared they'll make her get rid of it."

"And she doesn't want to?"

"No."

I tell him about Kerry's real father and how her mum stuck up for her.

When I stop he thinks for a minute then asks, "How

about your parents?"

On top of everything else, this is going to sound comic. It might be the plot from a soap opera.

"Well, actually…"

I tell him about Elaine, and about McCasky and Kitty.

At the end he says, "Not the best of times to add your news, then."

He's so dead-pan that I laugh. He smiles, too. But in the next minute an awful thought occurs.

"You won't tell them, will you?"

"No," he says. "Promise."

"Whew. Thanks."

He thinks for a minute, then says, "Given a totally free choice, what would you like to see happen?"

"You mean, right now? Or like, if things could be perfect?"

"Let's start with perfect."

"Kerry and me together, in some place of our own, with the baby. Only I'd need to be earning money and all that."

"What about right now?"

"I said I'd go back to school and really work. It was either that or stick in the DIY store and do a building apprenticeship."

"And further on?"

"University, I suppose. I was thinking I might do dentistry."

"Good choice if you want to make money."

I nod. There's a pause.

"What about your music?"

And that's the point. Will I want to spend my whole life sorting out people's grotty mouths? Bob and Liam and I could do paid gigs if we found another lead player. I thought Kerry might join us. Maybe she still can, later. I don't know. I put my hands over my face.

"It's a tough one, Cal," says Pirelli. "I can't make up your mind for you."

I shake my head.

"All I can say is, if you or Kerry need help at any point, let me know. I can put you in touch with people who do the practical stuff. Housing, that kind of thing. Continued education."

Oh, God. We're a statistic. Teenage pregnancy. Social workers. But he's doing his best.

"Thanks," I say.

He changes the subject.

"How's your sister getting on?"

"She's OK. She found a flat in Govan. It's near the river, she says. My father's buying it. He thinks that's the cheapest way, if I go to college as well. But I don't know."

"A lot can happen in a year," Pirelli points out. "It would be useful to get a decent Highers result, whatever else happens. You can do more if you pass exams than if you don't. Keep your options open."

That makes sense.

He glances at his watch, and gives me a regretful smile.

"This is a bad time to say goodbye, but as you know, I'm shifting on. Janet who replaces me is very nice. And she'll know all about it, you won't have to start from scratch."

I can't even nod.

He takes a card from his wallet and gives it to me.

"If things get desperate, phone me. Leave a message if I'm tied up and I'll get back to you."

Looks like I've been upgraded to Priority Nutter. Or maybe it's a downgrade.

I shove the card in my pocket and say, "Thanks."

He sees me out. At the door he asks, "Back to the island?"

"Not until tomorrow. Jess is playing in Princes Square with two other people. It's just kind of busking but…"

"Great. Enjoy your evening."

"Thanks."

I've said that word too often. It's stopped meaning anything.

Chapter 13

Princes Square is posh. Glass lifts, daylight coming through the roof, classy shops and cafes. The assembly area at the bottom is made of mosaic to look like water lilies and stuff, pretending it's a pool. There's a grand piano on the curving platform beside it.

Jess has teamed up with these two guys, drummer and keyboard player. She said that was the good thing about working at HMV, you got to meet a lot of music people. They're checking sound levels and chatting.

Jess sees me and comes over.

"OK?" she says. She means Pirelli I guess.

"Yeah, fine."

"Come and meet the guys."

I follow her onto the low platform by the pretend pool and she tells them, "This is my brother, Callum. Generally known as Cal. We've a band on the island."

The pianist turns from his stool and shakes hands. "I'm

Marty Grayson. Good you could come."

He's got a mic on the piano so he'll be doing vocals too. The drummer waves from behind the kit.

"That's Dave," says Marty. "Jess says you're into music?"

"Yeah. Guitar."

"We should have had you along."

Jess looks apologetic. "I did think of it," she tells me. "But you couldn't have made it to practice sessions."

"Sure."

It feels a bit weird, though, not being in there with them, tuning, checking levels, cracking jokes, the way you do.

About a dozen people are sitting on the wooden edge of the pool that isn't a pool, waiting for the music to start. I go and sit there, too.

I don't much like this place. There are layers of curving balconies going up to the glass roof, with cafe tables on them and shops behind. Can't see the people up there, but there's talk going on all over. Quite a few shops are boarded up now because of business being bad, but there are still people who look as if all they do is spend money and sit around with drinks and coffee and the kind of cakes you eat with a little fork.

Marty reaches for his mic and swivels round to announce the gig.

"Hi, everyone. Welcome to the newest trio on the block, *Lemongrass*. Featuring Jess McCasky on sax, Dave

Brigstock on drums and me, Marty Grayson, keyboard and vocals. Here's an old number you'll recognize, 'What Is This Thing Called Love'."

It's the Mingus version. Modern jazz, laid back, fast, intricate. Jess is good at this stuff, she sounds dead relaxed, never puts a foot wrong. One oldish guy is grooving away to it, clicking his fingers, shifting his shoulders like he'd dance if anyone encouraged him. Nobody does. Most of them look kind of take-it-or-leave-it. Mingus isn't easy. There's a scatter of applause at the end and the band go straight into "Blue Moon". Nothing fancy, just a smoochy ballad. Marty takes it in on piano then sings it. Not much of a voice, but nice easy timing. Jess comes in with the sax, plays the tune, then pretties it up. It goes down better than the Mingus, the older people really like it.

"Thank you," says Marty as the applause dies. "And now here's our take on a Thom Yorke song from his solo album, *The Eraser*. "It's called 'Atoms for Peace'."

A couple of girls shriek. Must be Radiohead fans. Marty gets the continuous riff going with his left hand then starts in on the vocal solo.

No more going to the dark side...

They've transposed it down a couple of tones because he can't sing as high as Thom does.

So many lies,
So many lies...

At the end, the girls who shrieked are clapping like

mad, but a couple of older people are walking out.

"For something quite different," says Marty, "here's another classic. 'Some of These Days'."

They do it very swingy, great sax stuff from Jess. Good choice. The audience loves it.

From the wholefood cafe on the top level, Elaine looked down at Jess playing her saxophone with her new friends and felt a glow of pride. She'd never imagined having a daughter who could stand in a public place so calmly, producing this intricate pattern of notes that so many people were listening to. Then she glanced at Andrew and wondered if he was putting up with it rather than enjoying it.

"Sorry if this isn't your sort of thing," she said.

Andrew smiled and said, "Death by modern jazz. It's OK. I'll survive. They're quite good, actually."

"Jess phoned to say they were playing. I couldn't think of an excuse not to come."

I want him to be all right about it.

"Yes, you said."

From up here, the music didn't sound too loud. Some people had started to dance on the mosaic floor that was meant to look like a lily pool. She stopped looking over the balcony and returned her attention to Andrew, but he was checking his phone.

He tapped in a reply, then said, "Interesting. A guy I knew back in the Lebanon days. He wants a photographer to work with him on a project about kids in an outer-city estate."

Oh, joy, Elaine thought.

She said, "Sounds interesting."

"I've done some stuff on them before," Andrew went on. "They're mostly Tunisian. They get the blame for every act of crime and vandalism, but it's not all their fault. The French have a bad streak of racial prejudice."

"French?"

"It's in Paris."

"Oh."

He ignored the doubt in her voice.

"It could be an answer to what we're going to do. I know you don't like my mother's house. Neither do I. It's a dismal little place. I should have done some refurbishing but looking after her was as much as I could cope with."

"Of course it was."

But he was right about the house. She couldn't see herself living in Kilmarnock with a betting shop on one side and a boarded-up ex-newsagents on the other.

"I should have put it up for sale straight after she died, I suppose. But I waited to see what would crop up."

"And what cropped up was me."

"It was indeed." He put his hand over hers. "And now we've the whole world to choose from."

"But – do you really want to leave Scotland?"

"I left Scotland years ago."

"I know. But where do you think of as home?"

He shrugged.

"Homes come and go. I've spent more time in the Middle East than anywhere."

"Andrew, I do not want to live in the Middle East."

"Fair enough."

He returned to the point.

"Do you know Paris?"

"Not really. I went there on a school trip when I was about thirteen. They took us to the Louvre but it was so packed with people, you couldn't see the pictures. And French toilets are disgusting."

"That was some time ago," Andrew pointed out. "They're much better now. And Paris really is a great city. Wonderful cafes, traditional French life still going on but very much at the heart of things."

"I'm not honestly that keen on cities."

"We could live in the outskirts if you wanted. Somewhere beyond the Bois de Boulogne."

She nodded and tried to look interested, but thought, *I am being railroaded.*

Her resistance surprised her. She'd thought the feeling of togetherness would be proof against anything like this.

Callum.

Yes, that was the trouble. The way he'd come to her in the garden like an older, more sensible boy and put his arms round her. The disappointment on his face when he said, "Oh. I thought you were staying."

There was a ripple of applause from below as the band finished a number. The pianist announced the next number and they started again.

"Andrew – I can't go flitting off to Paris."

"You flitted off to Greece."

"I know. But…"

"You wish you hadn't?"

"No! No, it was wonderful. I loved every minute."

But the colour had risen in her face. She looked down at the plate in front of her and flattened a couple of cake crumbs with the little fork, leaning her head on the other hand.

"Elaine, you have to be honest," Andrew said. "If you've gone off the whole thing, it's better to tell me now."

She put the fork down. *Honest.* What was it with men and this honesty thing? Couldn't they accept that we all have countless layers of feeling and commitment, and they shift around the whole time? Isn't it more useful to be nice than to be honest?

"I haven't gone off it," she said. "You've changed my life."

That was true.

The band segued into a smoochy rendering of "Autumn Leaves".

"Ah," Andrew said. "A great old number. *Les Feuilles d'Autonne.*"

And suddenly Elaine was irritated.

All very well for him, she thought. *He speaks French. And I don't even want to.*

There's these weird blue lights in Buchanan Street, like you're on the set of *Star Wars* or something. I don't know what that's about. People are still standing around in front of the entrance to Princes Square. Jess is with Marty, doing a postmortem about where she thinks the harmony detail wasn't right. I'm carting stuff for Dave. He's got a flat-pack kit so the drum-heads and cymbals fit into one case but there's the stands and his stool and stuff, and my rucksack.

Jess has stopped talking to Marty, she's hugging someone. Blonde hair...

It's Elaine. And a bloke in a crumpled jacket. Got to be him. Andrew bloody Adonis, the Greek geek.

Jess turns to him with a big smile and says, "Hi, Andrew, great you could make it." They shake hands. She does all that stuff so easily.

Elaine is on the wrong side of Jess and the geek, she can't get to me without circling round, but she's smiling at me kind of anxiously.

Dave says in my ear, "That your mum?"

I say, "Yeah."

I smile at Elaine and try to look like it's all normal. Not fair to dump Dave in the McCasky soap opera.

Elaine's worked her way round to join us.

"I thought you were excellent," she says to Dave. "And

you haven't been playing together long, have you?"

"We got together before Jess went to Malaysia," he says. "That's where the name came from. She came back raving about this stuff called lemongrass that they use in curries so we thought that would do."

Andrew's there, too.

"You'll be Callum," he says.

He has a shot at shaking hands but I'm holding Dave's stuff so it's a non-starter. His face looks like it got pebble-dashed.

"I'm Andrew Duncan," he says.

As if we didn't know.

He's staring at my hair. There's a bit of wind blowing down Buchanan Street so it's all over the place.

Elaine asks, as though we were alone together, "How did it go today?"

Everyone could hear. What am I supposed to say? *My shrink has written me off as a hopeless lunatic, he's put me on his emergency list.*

Jess comes to the rescue.

"Cal's been browsing the record shops," she says, laid back as ever. "And he's coming back to mine tonight."

She looks at Elaine very straight, and I know what she means, as if she'd put it in words. *Don't be so tactless. And anyway, where will you be tonight?*

Elaine looks away.

The Andrew person tries to lighten things up. "We're

going for a post-concert drink," he says. "Anyone like to join us?"

Jess says, "Not me, I'm afraid. I'd love to, but I'm working tomorrow, and it's getting late."

Marty and Dave say vague things like, "Yeah, bit late really."

I don't say anything.

"That's a shame," says Elaine. "But I hope we'll see you soon."

She kisses Jess. I retreat behind Dave and his drum case, out of kissing range, so she just gives me a sort of wave.

"Bye, darling. Take care of yourself."

"You too," I say.

Not that she needs to take care of herself, does she. Not when she's got dog-face looking after her.

"God, I'm knackered," says Jess.

She heads for the sofa and collapses. I know how she feels, it's always like that.

"Long gig," I say.

"Yeah. And we've not played together that long. No problem with the standard stuff, but when you start to get outside that, you want to be sure you're in touch."

"It sounded like you were," I say.

"Did it? That's good. We had a couple of hairy moments."

"I don't think they'd have noticed."

Jess knows what I mean. *They* are always the audience. With any luck they're keen, but they don't really understand what's going on.

I say, "Can I make you a coffee or something?"

It's only fair to offer. She's been working hard.

She hauls herself up and says, "I'm going to have a glass of wine. Marty brought a bottle round last night and there's some left. And before you start wondering – no, we're not an item. He's gay."

She goes into the little kitchen that opens off the living room. The flat still looks bare. There's just a sofa that makes into a bed, and a table and a couple of chairs. Lots of cardboard boxes – she hasn't finished unpacking yet. I follow her into the kitchen, but there's hardly room for both of us, with the fridge and washing machine close up on one side and the cooker and cupboards on the other. She splits what's left in the wine bottle between two glasses and gives me one without asking. I'm not used to wine, really. The cough-mixture taste of it gets to the back of my throat a bit, but I can feel its warmth going down and spreading through me. I can see why she didn't want coffee.

"You must be hungry," she says. "Did you come straight from the tyres man to the gig?"

"Yes."

Actually, I'm ravenous. I haven't eaten anything since a bacon butty on the boat. There were all those food smells in Princes Square, curry and goulash and stuff, but the prices were ridiculous.

"How about beans on toast?" Jess says. "I haven't got much else."

"Brilliant."

How are Kerry and I going to live? Everything costs money.

Jess puts four slices of bread in the toaster and hands me a tin of beans. "Stick those in a saucepan," she says. "There's one in the cupboard beside you."

It's a gas cooker, and I can't see how to light it. We use matches for the propane stove in the bothy.

"Turn the ring on and press the lighter button," Jess says.

The good thing about beans on toast is, they're quick. We carry the plates to the table in the living room and get stuck in.

When we've finished, Jess finds a couple of bananas and some biscuits, then she makes coffee, and we're back on the sofa.

"So how are you doing?" she asks. "How's Kerry?"

The question catches me unprepared. Just for a moment, I was so warm and comfortable, I'd stopped thinking about it.

"She's OK."

Jess looks at me rather carefully.

"And you're happy?" she asks.

It's nice of her to care. I'm struggling to know what to

say. I've always told Jess everything, but this is different.

She puts her hand on my knee.

"Cal. Honeybun. What's the matter? Tell me."

I shake my head.

"Is it Pop? Is he being awful?"

Another shake. I'm swallowing hard, but the ache in my throat won't go away.

"Is it about Elaine?"

"Not really."

The words come out at the wrong pitch, too high.

Jess puts both hands round her coffee mug, looking at me.

"If you can't tell me," she says, "I'll have to guess, won't I?"

I can't even nod.

"Kerry's ditched you?"

"No!"

"Well," Jess says, "the only other thing I can think of is, she's pregnant."

The worry and secrecy of it overflows. I give a small nod. And it's too much.

Jess rescues the coffee mug before it spills, and puts it on the floor. She puts her arm round my shoulders.

"Cheer up, cuckoo," she says. "It's not the end of the world."

But it is. I promised Kerry I wouldn't tell. I've let her down.

A key scratches in the outside door.

In comes Mairi. That's all I need.

"Hi," she says. "Did you have a good gig?"

I bolt into the bathroom.

By the time I come out, Mairi's sitting beside Jess, where I was. The pair of them look at me with concern.

"That's really bad luck, Cal," says Mairi.

So Jess has told her. I really have blown it.

"Please don't tell anyone," I beg.

"Of course we won't," Jess says at once.

Mairi makes a zip gesture across her mouth and says, "Not a word."

But I feel cold inside.

Chapter 14

It's weird, being back at school. So normal, but nothing's normal.

After biology, Kerry and I faff about with books and things until the others have gone out. We don't want to be seen around together too much, but I worry about her all the time.

"You OK?" I ask.

"Not really. All I want is oranges."

"They've got fruit in the cafeteria. I'll get you one."

"Don't bother just now."

She perches on the edge of a table.

"Mum knows I was sick the other morning. She said she was going to phone the medical centre but I talked her out of it."

"I wish I could take care of you. I wish we were older."

"Well, we're not," she says flatly.

If only I could ditch school, I could be getting on with

the bothy. I lugged half a roll of roofing felt up there last week and nailed it on the rotting timbers as best I could. Difficult without a ladder, the joists kept breaking away. I need more time.

What are we going to do? We can't keep it secret forever.

"Do you think your mum suspects?" I ask.

"I guess she does. But it's a hard thing to ask, isn't it. I mean, if she asked if I was pregnant and I wasn't, I'd be furious."

It's awful, this waiting for I don't know what. I wish whatever's going to happen would start happening.

No I don't, that's stupid, it'll probably be worse.

"It's just I want to hang on as long as I can," Kerry says. "Otherwise I know what Derek will say. *Get it fixed, right now*. And Mum would go along with it."

"You reckon?"

"Yes, she would. She's my mum and she loves me, I know she does. But she feels bad about what happened. She wouldn't hurt him again. So it's down to me."

She takes a deep breath.

"I don't buy this stuff about a baby not being alive until it's big enough to start moving. You and me, we're both alive, and the stuff we're made of is alive. My egg was alive when I made it and so was the sperm you made." She puts a hand on her school sweatshirt where it covers the top of her trousers, like she's defending what's in there. "This baby has been alive from the first moment."

It's awful to feel so useless.

She looks at the clock and gets up from the table.

"Better go."

"What have you got next?"

"French."

I look outside and there's nobody. I put my hand out to her and she grips it tightly, and turns her head to give me a kiss. Then she goes away down the corridor with her bag over her shoulder, dark green sweatshirt, black trousers, like an ordinary sixth-year girl. And all I can do is watch her.

The Goth collars me at the top of the stairs to Technology. She's smiling.

"Callum, I haven't seen you since we've been back. I'm so pleased that you decided to stay on. It's a really sensible decision, and I'm sure you won't regret it."

Nice that someone's sure about something.

"Are you happy with the timetable? No problems about subjects overlapping?"

"It's fine."

I haven't looked at the timetable. Can't be bothered. I just hang on in with the rest of the group. I don't mind getting stuck into the homework. It gives me a good excuse to keep out of the way. Kitty isn't in the house any more, but Elaine isn't, either. I don't want to get stuck with McCasky when he's got nobody else to talk to. He's not in the best of moods now Kitty's gone.

Mrs Mack lowers her voice and says, "I'm so sorry to hear about your family problems."

My face flares. She *knows*.

"I do hope your father is coping," she goes on.

Whew. She means the Elaine thing. That'll be the talk of the island, of course. They've got another treat coming, though. Just wait until my bit of news breaks. I shut my eyes for a moment in horror at the thought, and the Goth gets an overdose of insight.

"I'm so sorry. I didn't mean to be tactless."

She looks like she'll put her hand on my arm, then she remembers I might sue her for making advances to an innocent boy, so she doesn't. There's a laugh in there somewhere.

I shake my hair back and give her the neutral look I learned from Pirelli.

"It's OK," I assure her. "I think my parents are both kind of – happy."

She's knocked out.

"Oh, Callum. That's a very *mature* thing to say. So brave of you. But if there's any way in which I can help, don't hesitate to ask."

"Sure. Thanks."

She's going to be sick as a parrot when she hears.

I spoke to him just the other day, and he never said a word.

* * *

There's a spider on the bus, up at the top of the window. Not a good place for a spider. There's nothing to eat except for the odd midge, and it can't spin properly in here. If it starts a web it'll just get broken, and sooner or later it'll be squashed or else hoovered up when the bus gets cleaned. I suppose they do clean the buses sometimes.

If the windows opened I'd let the spider out, but they don't, so it'll have to wait until Kilkeddie. I'll keep an eye on it so I know where it is when we get there.

Spiders live on their own, in webs that are their homes as well as food-catchers. They can make webs from when they're quite tiny. They don't have to pass Higher Spinning. They hatch out of one of those yellow cocoons stuck into a corner somewhere and get on with it. How do they know how to do that?

Elaine used to read a book called the *Just So Stories* to us when Jess and I were small. Rudyard Kipling. There was one about the Eldest Magician, who told the animals what game they were to play. The elephant played at being an elephant and the cow played at being a cow and so on, and they all showed him how they were playing and said, "*Kun?*" meaning, "Right?" and the Eldest Magician said "*Payah kun.*" "Quite right." There was only one animal that wouldn't play, and that was the man, because he thought he was better than all the others. I wonder if we've still got that book. It had gold letters and an elephant's head in a circle on the front.

I never knew how much I liked being told stories. I wish I could be small again. I want to believe the grown-ups look after everything and I've nothing to do but play in the sun.

I lean my head against the bus window. If it was soft I might cry, but the glass bumps and keeps things practical. Anyway, I need to watch the spider so I can pick it up when we get to Kilkeddie and put it in a better place. Then it can get on with playing at being a spider. *Payah kun.*

Elaine fished the camomile teabag out of a mug of hot water and dropped it in the bin. She looked round the poky kitchen with its powder-blue hardboard units and stained aluminium saucepans with no lids and thought. *Nobody's cooked in here for years. Meals on Wheels, I suppose.* Since she'd been here, they'd eaten out or bought picnic stuff. Andrew's mother's bed still stood in the dining room. There were white grab-rails screwed onto every wall on the ground floor, and her wheelchair was folded up beside the front door that led straight out onto the pavement.

She added some milk to the coffee she'd made for Andrew and carried it through to him in the sitting room. He was still looking at houses in Paris, in spite of their conversation at Jess's concert.

"Thanks," he said, then turned the laptop to show her. "What about this?"

A tall house with narrow shutters and a small balcony above the front door.

"Have I seen that one before?" she asked.

"No. Eight rooms, terrace at the back, nice views. What do you think?"

I can't go to France. I thought he understood. What can I say?

"It's kind of … hard to imagine."

"You don't have to imagine. It's a photograph."

"Living there, I mean. What it would be like."

"You can't know things in advance. I didn't know what looking after my mother would be like."

"Was it awful, really? You've never said."

Andrew glanced back at the screen, then sighed and turned back to her.

"When I was discharged from hospital she looked after me. For weeks. It can't have been easy. Not just the nursing care, mentally I was a mess. Black moods, fury, convinced I was finished and done for. She put up with all that. Kept it to herself that she had cancer symptoms, never said a word."

"Heavens. When did you find out?"

"I went to the kitchen door one day and she was standing at the sink, didn't know I was there. She had her hands pressed against her back as if she was in pain."

"What was it?"

"Kidney cancer. It moved fast. Within a few months, she needed me more than I needed her."

Maybe the heaviness of this small Kilmarnock house comes from that. Too much duty. Too much love. Can you have too much love?

Andrew clicked the picture off.

"The job in France is a no-no, isn't it? You want to stay here because of Callum. Right?"

"Well – yes."

"So what am *I* supposed to do?"

He's getting more like Fergus by the minute, Elaine thought. *Have I turned him into a Fergus?* She pushed the thought away.

"I feel as if I'm two people," she said. "One of them is with you, absolutely. But the other – you're right. Callum finds the real world hard to cope with."

"And you think you can help him with that?"

"Maybe not. But I can't let him think I don't care."

Andrew's lips tightened slightly.

"You haven't answered my question. Where do I come in? Or don't I?"

Go on seeing Andrew if you want. Fergus must have known it was impossible. That's why he could make the offer.

She had to try, though. It was the last card she could play.

"You're right. I can't leave. But I want to go on seeing you."

The words were jumping in her mind and she couldn't seem to get a proper breath.

"Fergus said..." She couldn't find the right words. "He wouldn't mind. I mean, if I saw you here sometimes. Or – if you came to the island. I mean, there are some lovely houses..."

Andrew looked at her in blank astonishment. Then he gave a kind of laugh.

"You really think I'd settle for that? As your piece on the side, your – your *spare man*? With everyone laughing behind my back? Elaine, I really do find that rather extraordinary."

"I'm sorry. I shouldn't have – it was stupid."

Andrew closed his laptop, unplugged it and rammed it into its black travel case, pushed the flex in as well, zipped the case shut. The loss that had now been made certain spread sadness through the small room.

After a few minutes Elaine said, "Please. I really am sorry."

He looked at his own fingers, gripping the black case.

"These weeks have been very good," he said. "Perhaps the best of my life. I thank you for that. But you must go your own way now."

Elaine nodded.

Somewhere at the depths of her being, she found a strange relief.

McCasky's phone rings. We're watching TV over coffee after some sort of meal.

"Well, hi," he says. "Hang on a minute."

He takes the phone upstairs.

Got to be Elaine. I stay where I am. I was going to go up and play my guitar, but I don't want him to think I'm trying to listen. He's up there for quite a long time. When he comes down, he says, "That's your mother coming back."

"To stay?"

"Far as I know. She'll be on the afternoon boat tomorrow."

I nod. Don't know what to say. Will it really be OK?

He pours himself a whisky and puts on this CD of the pop stuff he plays when he's in a good mood. Cat Stevens, "Morning Has Broken". Bit of a cheat, really – it's just an old hymn tune. It was the Rick Wakeman piano bit that really got to people. McCasky's tapping his fingers to it, on the arm of his leather chair. *Old Pop and his old pops*, as Jess says.

I go up to my room. Downstairs, the music has shifted to something else, but I work out the Wakeman thing on my guitar. I can see why it sold millions.

After a bit I call Jess, but her phone's engaged.

I play a bit more then try again, but it's still engaged. Maybe McCasky is telling her the news about Elaine.

Chapter 15

The repair I did to the bothy roof hasn't worked. Most of the felt blew off in last night's wind. One section is still up there but the rest is lying on the stones outside where the top of the wall collapsed years ago.

Trouble is, I'm going to need a ladder. I can't smuggle one of those out of the yard. I climbed up the elder tree when I nailed the stuff on, but the branches kept breaking away. Kerry was looking up at me and saying, "Oh, do be careful." Not a lot of help.

She isn't here yet. I've put the kettle on the camping gas stove. She might like a hot drink when she gets here. Probably just hot water. She's gone off tea and coffee.

I'm sitting in the doorway with my feet in the grass. It's still breezy after the windy night, but the sun's shining. A good Sunday morning.

Kerry's coming up the hill now, I can hear her footsteps. Bit slower than usual, I hope she's feeling OK. The kettle boils, nice timing. It's got this whistle on its spout – a high B-flat. I go in and turn the gas down and reach for a couple of mugs. Kerry's at the door so I say, "Hi," and turn my head to smile at her—

Oh, my God.

It's not Kerry. It's McCasky.

He doesn't say anything, just looks all round with his fists on his hips. Walks across and stares up at the hole in the roof and the one bit of felt that's still dangling from a beam.

"No use tacking stuff on rotten wood," he says.

"I *know*."

What's he doing here? Has Bill told him about the stuff I've been lifting from the scrap store? He needn't worry, I've put the money in the till for it.

He says, "I'll have a coffee if you're making one."

"There's only powdered milk."

"That'll do."

He's looking at the table I've made, and the bench. And the stack of four-by-two I've been piling up against the wall, ready to do the roof when I can.

"I've paid for everything," I say.

"I know you have."

He comes over and picks up his mug of coffee.

"So what's the plan?" he asks. "What are you trying to do here?"

"Just – somewhere to shelter when it's raining."

If he thinks I'm going to tell him all our private dreams, he must be joking. I wait for him to give me hell about ducking the question, but he just says, "Got any sugar?"

I hand him the screw-top jar. We had sugar in a packet but the ants got into it. We scooped the ant-free sugar into a jar and put the rest outside for them to finish. Kerry said they must have thought they'd died and gone to heaven.

McCasky stirs his coffee, then puts the spoon down on the plastic tray we call the draining board.

"Did you check who this place belongs to?" he asks.

I'm gobsmacked.

I thought old ruins didn't belong to anyone. I thought whoever once owned the bothy was long dead and didn't know or care if its roof fell in. But McCasky will know, of course. He knows everything. He's come to tell me we're in someone else's property and we have to get out. I hate him.

He takes a leisured sip of coffee.

"It's mine," he says. "I bought it when Willie Geraghty died. Got it for next to nothing."

"I didn't know."

"Aye, well, you wouldn't."

I don't know why he's not bawling me out like he usually does. He starts back at the beginning.

"So what's the plan?"

"Don't have one."

And that does it.

He slams the coffee mug down on the tray and shouts,

"Fuck's sake, boy, *why* don't you have a plan? You stand there looking like a bloody chrysanthemum and tell me you've no idea what you're doing? Can't you even *admit* you're in deep shit?"

What does he mean, "deep shit"? What does he know?

He looks away for a minute then takes a breath. Back in control.

"Look, Cal, cards on the table. You've got this lassie pregnant. And from what I hear, she intends to go through with it. So when I ask you what your plan is, I want an answer."

My hands are over my face. I can't look at him, I want to be in darkness forever. Mairi talked, didn't she? I knew she would. The whole island will be gossiping. I've let Kerry down. Oh, God.

McCasky turns his head and says, "Come in."

What? Oh, Jeez, Kerry's at the door. She doesn't know who he is, she's backing away.

"It's OK," I say. "This is – er – my dad."

I've never called him that, even to her. She stares at me and stays where she is.

"Coffee?" McCasky asks her, as if he owns the place. Which, of course, he does.

She looks at him, then at me.

"I didn't know he was coming," I say.

She nods. Then walks in and says, "Great to meet you. Just hot water, please." Totally calm. I don't know how she can be.

McCasky gives her a nod of respect and they shake hands like this was some kind of business meeting.

"Why don't you sit down," he says.

Kerry sits in one of the camping chairs. I hand her a mug of hot water and McCasky points me towards the chair beside her. I take Kerry's hand, trying to warn her what he's going to say.

He doesn't waste any time.

"If what I hear is true," he says, "and I'm sure it is – you're in quite a fix, the pair of you." He looks at Kerry. "You're expecting a bairn, right?"

How does he *know*?

Her fingers clutch mine and she gives a small gasp, but she faces him bravely.

"Yes."

"How far on are you?"

"I've just missed a second time."

"You want to keep it?"

"Yes."

"Have you told your parents?"

She shakes her head.

"Well, lassie," he says, quite kindly, "they'll have to know."

And her calmness cracks up. She's struggling not to cry. She presses the back of her hand against her nose. After a minute, she manages to speak.

"Does everyone know?"

"Not yet."

McCasky shifts his attention to me.

"You'll be wondering how I know. Jess phoned this morning. I'd have told you, but you'd already gone out."

Jess. Not Mairi, *Jess.* I can't believe it. And who else?

"Does Elaine know?"

"Yes. She phoned Jess last night to say she was coming back here. And Jess told her."

So that's why her phone was engaged.

She promised she wouldn't tell.

She *promised.* I trusted her.

Who can you trust? Nobody.

I get up and blunder out through the grass and brambles and lean against the unreliable elder tree.

I feel cold and sick.

Elaine gazed out of the train window. Each station that went past was more like the proper countryside. Trees and winding roads, open fields, narrow footbridges at unmanned stations. A comforting landscape. *Make the most of it*, she thought. After Callum's bombshell, all sorts of upheavals lay ahead.

Her phone rang.

"Hi," Jess said. "You on your way to the ferry?"

"Yes. I'm on the train."

"Have you heard from Pop?"

"Not today, no. Did you tell him about Kerry?"

"Yes. First thing this morning. I couldn't face it last night. Telling one parent had been enough."

Elaine was hurt.

"I don't think I was particularly difficult."

"'Course you weren't. I didn't mean that. Just – there's a bit of psyching up involved, you know? And he's better in the mornings. Work mode, all that."

"So you've actually told him?"

"Yes."

"How did he take it?"

"Pretty good, really. He said he wasn't surprised."

"Was Callum there?"

"No, Pop said he'd gone out. He thought he might be up in the bothy. He was going up there right away. Said he had to talk to him."

"Oh, dear."

"Well, there's got to be some talking sooner or later."

"I know. You're absolutely right. But—"

Jess cut in.

"I feel so awful about telling. I promised Cal I wouldn't. He's going to be totally gutted. I know it was a let-down, but I'd thought and thought about it, and I couldn't see that shutting up was going to help."

"I'm glad you did. It would have to be said sooner or later."

"Yes, but – you know what he's like. He does things his own way."

"I know. It's so hard to see how to help him."

After a pause, Jess said, "And there's Kerry's family. They'll need to know, too, but I guess that's down to her." Then she added, "I told you she has a different father, didn't I?"

"You mean, not the outdoor shop man? No, you didn't."

"Sorry. I thought I had. It was when I came home that time, and heard her playing with Cal and the boys. Her real dad's an Australian Aboriginal. That's why she can play that fantastic music."

"Oh, my goodness. Fergus was right, then. He said she looked like that the first time we saw her, at the end of the summer concert. Doesn't it seem a long time ago?"

Jess was not to be deflected.

"Mairi bought a pair of trainers from the guy at the outdoor shop. She said he's all muscle and no brain."

How intolerant young people can be.

"Oh, Jessica. He's probably kind at heart."

Jess sighed. "You know your trouble?" she said. "You try to be too nice. Look, I've got to go, I'm meeting someone. Call me this evening, yeah? Let me know how it goes?"

"I will do," said Elaine. "And thanks, darling. I'm sure you did the right thing."

"Fingers crossed," said Jess. "Bye."

McCasky comes out to the elder tree. He puts his hand on my shoulder.

"There are worse things," he says. "Nobody's died."

Somehow, I don't feel scared of him. Maybe I've gone past that.

"Half the kids in the country are born to people who aren't married," he goes on.

I nod dumbly. But being married isn't the point.

McCasky's hand is still on my shoulder. He rubs his thumb across it gently. I find I've made a stupid noise, like a kind of sob.

"Hey," he says. "Come on."

He slides his arm across my shoulders and pulls me close. He's so strong, he could crush my ribs. But he gives my back a couple of pats like I was a kid with hiccups and leaves it at that.

"The house could do with a tidy up," he says. "With your mother coming back."

He means, he needs some help. Without Kitty there, the place is a tip.

"OK," I say.

"No hurry. Take your time."

And he's off down the hill. I go back into the bothy.

Kerry's lit the gas under the kettle again. She's standing with her hands over it as if she's cold. She turns to me and I hold her close. Her face is buried against my neck and I can hardly hear what she says.

"I'm sorry."

"What d'you mean?"

"I've made such a mess of it all. You're going to hate me."

"I'll never hate you."

She refills her mug with hot water and we sit down on the bench.

"Cal," she says, and her words come out in a rush. "Listen. If it's all too much – you've got to say. I wouldn't let anyone else talk me out of it, but if you really can't bear the idea of this baby – I'll have an abortion. I wouldn't for Derek or anyone, but…"

She can't go on.

For me, she would stop this small life, and everything could go back to the way it was.

There's just one flash of tantalizing freedom, but it's gone.

If I ask her to do that, we'll both have to live with knowing it. For ever. I don't think she'd stay. I'm not even sure I would.

Kerry's hand is over her face. The mug in her other hand is tilting, and water is dribbling onto the floor. I rescue it.

"No," I say. "This baby is ours. We made it. Both of us."

"Cal – are you sure?"

The final pause is no more than a second.

"Yes," I say. "I'm sure."

Chapter 16

McCasky's got the washing machine on and he's ironing a shirt.

"What's this – slave labour?" he says when he sees Kerry.

"No, I'm just the audience," she says.

But when I haul the vacuum cleaner out of the cupboard she takes it from me and says, "I'll do that. You do the tidying – I don't know where things go."

I'm not sure she ought to be doing energetic stuff like vacuuming.

"You all right for this? You're not feeling sick or anything?"

She shrugs and says, "Moving around doesn't make it any worse."

And she plugs the machine in and starts on the sitting-room carpet.

I dump some old magazines in the bin and go upstairs with my arms full of newer ones and some trainers and socks. My room looks like a bomb site, but I shove everything into cupboards and gather up the dirty coffee mugs and clothes. I carry them down to the kitchen.

When I open the dishwasher, a blast of hot air comes out because it's just finished.

"You could put that clean stuff away," McCasky says.

So I do that. Then the washing machine comes to a stop so I bundle the wet stuff into the laundry basket and set a new lot going, then cart the basket into the garden. Does Elaine peg T-shirts up by the shoulders or the bottom edge? Guess it doesn't matter.

When I get back into the house Kerry's moved into the dining room with the vacuum cleaner.

"That table could do with a wipe," she says, shouting over its noise.

I get a damp cloth from the kitchen.

McCasky's on the last shirt.

I'm not in the habit of speaking to him voluntarily, but on the way down the hill Kerry and I decided what to do, and he'll have to know.

"We're going to Kerry's house after we've finished here," I say. "We – I mean, she says she's got to tell them."

"Good."

He hangs the shirt up and unplugs the iron.

Then he says, "If you want to do that now, I'll finish off here."

I'd been thinking we'd go down there in about an hour, but he's turned it into this minute.

"Well, if that's OK," I say.

"Wouldn't have said if it wasn't."

He folds up the ironing board and takes it out to put in the hall cupboard. Kerry's looping the flex round the cleaner to carry it upstairs.

"Leave that, Kerry," he says, "Thanks for your help. You go and do what you have to."

She looks at me and I shrug. He's in charge.

"Oh," she says. "Right."

Kerry's wee brothers are out in the garden, playing some sort of traffic game with a pedal car and a plastic tennis racket. Her mother is at the kitchen sink, peeling potatoes.

"Mum, this is Cal," says Kerry.

She looks up and smiles. I remember her from the boat, brown hair in a ponytail. She's wearing jeans and a blue top that's got dark marks where the potato water has splashed.

"How nice to meet you!" she says. She grabs a towel for a quick wipe then shakes my hand. "I've been hoping Kerry would bring you home at some point. I'm Louise."

She tips her head towards the television sound from the next room.

"Derek's watching the cricket. Best not to disturb him until it's over. Would you like some tea? Coffee? A cold drink?"

"Just water," says Kerry, and I say, "Me, too."

It's true. My throat feels clammed up because of what we have to say.

Kerry fills a couple of glasses from the tap. She hands me one and gives me a very straight look. I know what she means. It's got to be now, before he comes in.

She puts her glass down on the table.

"Mum," she says. "We have to tell you something."

Her mother turns from the sink.

"What is it?"

But the look on her face says she knows.

Everything goes wobbly. Kerry's trying to find words.

"I'm…"

She can't go any further. She crams a hand over her face and starts to cry.

Louise hugs her close.

"Oh, darling," she says. "I was afraid you were."

She looks at me across Kerry's head while she goes on holding her. I don't know what the look means. It isn't angry, more kind of curious, as if she's trying to know what sort of person this boy with the crazy orange hair is. I expect she thinks I'm useless. *A bloody chrysanthemum*, like McCasky said.

"I – want to look after her," I say.

"Well," she says, "that won't be easy for you, will it?"

She doesn't have any trace of Australian accent in spite of being out there so long. She's just Scottish. She came from here. It makes her closer. It makes it worse. She reaches for a tissue and hands it to Kerry, and asks her gently, "When's it due?"

"Early April."

"Why didn't you tell me?"

Kerry takes a shivering breath.

"Because Derek would say I'd to get rid of it. But I want it, Mum. It's mine."

Louise looks at me across Kerry's head and asks, "What about you?"

I say, "I want it, too."

There's a blast of music from the TV. All three of us look in its direction, knowing what it means. The cricket has ended. The kitchen door opens and Derek comes in. He chucks an empty lager can in the bin and says, "Can ya believe it. Fucking Poms have won."

Then he notices something's going on.

"Trouble?" he asks.

Louise comes straight out with it.

"Derek. Kerry is pregnant," she says.

No other way to put it, I suppose, but his face flushes red.

"Jesus," he says, and looks at me. "This your doing?"

"Cal had the courage to come with Kerry and tell us," says Louise.

"Whaddya mean, *courage*? He comes round here and says he's knocked my daughter up and you call it *courage*?"

She's not your daughter, I think, but I don't say it. I don't say anything. Neither does anyone else. Louise has put her arm round Kerry as if to protect her.

Derek takes a step towards me, chin jutting. His fists are clenched. I manage not to take a step back, but I duck my head because I think he's going to hit me.

"Look at him anyway, what a fucking pansy. Couldn't she have found herself a proper man?"

He shifts his glare to Kerry. "As to you – I mighta known it. You been trouble from the start." Then he adds to Louise, "All I can say is, take her down the doc's first thing tomorrow and get it fixed."

Louise doesn't say anything. She looks at me. I take a deep breath.

"We want to keep it."

He gives a bark of laughter.

"Oh, do you? Right, if you're so bloody cocky, you keep it. You keep *her*. You earn the money, buy her a house and a pram and all the fucking baby clothes. You're welcome. She's all yours, I wash my hands of her. And by the time you're finished, you'll wish you'd kept your fly zipped."

His words are like being hit repeatedly over the head. Some part of my mind is wondering why Louise married him. She seems so nice.

Kerry comes to stand beside me. I take her hand, and our fingers lace together tightly.

She faces Derek and says, "I knew you'd say that. All right, then. We'll manage."

She heads for the door and I follow her.

"Kerry, wait!" says Louise.

"We'll talk later, Mum," Kerry says without looking back.

Outside, the little boys are still playing their game. Either they haven't heard the raised voices or they're used to them. Kerry pauses and looks at them.

I'm scared she might give in and go on being their big sister who's always there.

"Keep going," I say.

And she does.

When we get back, the house is empty. McCasky will have gone to meet Elaine at the pier. Kerry hasn't said much on the way back. Neither have I. The things Derek shouted at us are probably running in her head, same as they are in mine.

Everything looks brilliantly clean and tidy. I ask, "Are you hungry?"

"I am, actually," Kerry says. "I felt awful before, but now I'm ravenous." She spots the fruit bowl. "Oranges. Can I have one?"

"Of course."

She starts peeling it straight away. I can't be bothered with oranges, they're too much trouble.

There's a pizza in the fridge but it's probably meant for later. I get out some cheese and a packet of ham. There's plenty of bread.

Kerry's nearly finished her orange.

"Would you like a toastie?" I ask.

We've got a machine that makes them like cafes do, with dark brown stripes.

She says, "Yes, please. Just cheese though, not ham. Have you got any pickle?"

"Think so. In that cupboard, behind you."

She washes her fingers under the tap then looks.

"Got it."

Eating is so good when you're really hungry.

I mop up the cheese that dribbled out with the last of the toastie. I want to ask the question that's been bugging me.

"Why did your mum marry Derek?"

I'd thought McCasky was bad, but Derek's definitely worse.

Kerry shrugs. "She loved him. She says he used to be so funny and nice. Great at sport. And he was really good looking. He had his hair quite long then, parted on one side with a cow-lick that flopped over his eyes like an old-fashioned Pommy cricket player. Dead classy. I've seen the photos."

Floppy cow-lick. Yeah, that would be better. Now he just looks bald.

Kerry says, "It was me being born that screwed everything up. This your compost bin?"

"Yes."

She drops her orange peels in, washes her hands and starts clearing the table.

"You didn't ask to be born," I say. "If it hadn't been you, he'd have found something else to be horrible about."

"He's nice sometimes. He's a good dad to the boys, plays with them and all that. They think he's great."

If she can't go back home, where's she going to live? What's she going to do for money? Derek's right, I can't help. Can she get an allowance or anything? *I can put you in touch with people*, Pirelli said. I almost want to pick up the phone and call him right now. But Elaine and McCasky will be on their way back. They may be here any minute.

"Does your mum like cut flowers?" Kerry asks. "There's masses of sweet peas by the fence."

"Don't know. She might."

Elaine's secateurs are on the shelf by the back door. We go out and gather sweet peas. I cut them because I can reach higher, and Kerry holds them. Thin stalks, blossoms as bright as silk against her dark skin. Purple, mauve, red, pink. Their scent is wonderful.

"That'll do," Kerry says. "I'll find something to put them in."

She goes ahead of me into the house. I don't hurry. When this moment of blossom and scent ends, everything is going to be different.

McCasky's pick-up is still standing in the yard. He's taken Elaine's Polo, then. And as though I've dreamed it, the car turns in off the road. He backs it into its parking place, fast like he always does, and kills the engine.

McCasky slams the boot shut, he's carting the stuff in, bags in both hands. Elaine looks up and sees me. She waves. She's running up the steps towards me, pale hair bright in the sun. We meet at the end of a row of overgrown peas and hug.

"Callum," she says.

She's never called me Cal. Time she did.

It's not a surprise this time, but I say, "I like your hair."

"Do you? Oh, good. But how are *you*?"

"Fine."

I'd better warn her.

"Kerry's here."

"Oh. Goodness."

Not the best thing to say, but she changes it quickly.

"What a good idea. So much better than…"

She's stuck for words, so I have to rescue her.

"Yeah. That's what we thought."

We go down to the house.

Kerry's in the kitchen, wiping the draining board. I don't know where McCasky is. Watching TV, probably.

Elaine says, "Kerry," same as she said my name when she saw me.

There's a bit of a dither about whether they shake hands or hug, but it settles as a handshake and the nice-to-meet-you stuff. Then it all goes a bit sticky.

Kerry says, "I've put the kettle on."

"Oh, isn't that sensible," says Elaine.

I say, "Why don't you go and sit down. We'll bring it through."

She doesn't like that idea. "It's all right, I'll do it."

"Please," says Kerry. "We'd like to."

"Oh. Well – thank you."

When we go in with the tray, she's grouped the chairs round the coffee table. And the TV is off. McCasky is looking out of the window with his hands in his pockets.

After the pouring-out and the handing round of biscuits, Elaine does a bit of chit-chat. Do you like living on the island, isn't it very different from Australia, all that stuff. When it peters out, McCasky looks at Kerry and says, "So what's the story at home?"

"My stepfather is furious," Kerry says.

"Has he thrown you out?"

Kerry and I look at each other. We're not quite sure.

I put my hair back from my face and tell him, "He said it was up to me to look after her. Like, find a house. Provide money and everything."

McCasky ignores that. He asks Kerry, "Can you go home tonight?"

"I don't know."

"Fergus, we can't let her go back," Elaine says. "This man might be violent."

"I doubt it," says McCasky, and gets up from his chair. "I'll go and see him."

"Do be careful," says Elaine.

He doesn't even look back. If anyone knows how to walk out of a room, it's McCasky.

"Oh, my God," says Kerry.

Elaine does a bit of soothing. "Sometimes it's best to leave the men to do their head-to-head bit. Don't worry, I'm sure Fergus will sort it out."

Kerry and I don't say anything.

Elaine ploughs on.

"I'm just concerned about the future. You and Callum will need somewhere to live."

Kerry says, "We'll just have to do what we can."

"Sometimes things work out for the best, if you just wait."

"Yes. Could be things are, like, 'meant'."

They get into conversation about fate.

Jingle, the remaining cat, comes in, though neither of them notices. Elaine never liked him as much as Barnaby. He rubs against me then sits down, looking round. He hasn't had much of a time of it lately, either. I put my hand down and stroke him. The conversation between Kerry and Elaine goes on. And I go on stroking.

Chapter 17

This was what Elaine had been looking forward to, picking tomatoes and smelling their sharp, sweet scent. Green stains on her fingers that would make the water from the tap run yellow until they were clean. Light still spreading through the cool sky though the sun was behind the hill.

Callum and the girl she had started to think of as a new daughter were in the kitchen. Kerry was chopping onions. She seemed very practical. And of course, she was lovely to look at. So dark. So vibrant. Very *real*. Easy to understand how Cal had been bewitched.

The garden was in better shape than she'd expected. Kitty Reed must have done a bit. Blast her. There were signs that the rows of carrots and beetroot had been weeded, and there weren't too many peas turning dry and wrinkled on the plants. The lettuces had bolted, but the peppers were cropping well. And the cucumbers had gone crazy. She'd grown the short outdoor kind this year, and look at the result – hundreds of them. And it seemed no time since she had pushed the seeds edgeways into their pots of compost, back in the spring. A crazy harvest, indeed.

"Which saucepan does your mum use?" Kerry asks.

I hand her one and she sets it on the stove, pours some oil in, then scrapes the onions in from the board and gives them a stir. She looks as if she's done it before, lots of times.

Elaine comes in with her basket of tomatoes and stuff.

"Oh, good," she says. "You've got the sauce started."

"Shall I do some salad?" asks Kerry.

"That would be good. Just look at all these cucumbers. We can have tzatziki."

"What's that?"

"It's a Greek cucumber salad with yogurt. Delicious."

I'm careful not to look at Kerry. We never had anything Greek before.

In the silence, we hear McCasky's pick-up pull into the yard. He comes in and gets a can of beer out of the fridge. I know better than to ask him something until he's ready, but Elaine can't wait.

"How did you get on?"

He takes a drink from the can and nods at Kerry. "You'll be all right to go back home."

Kerry says, "Oh. OK. Thanks." Then gets on with peeling garlic.

Elaine isn't satisfied. "Yes, but Fergus, what did he *say*?"

McCasky shrugs. "What you'd expect. Bringing disgrace on the family. Ruining his reputation, wrecking his business. He wants to send her back to Australia to stay with his mother."

"I knew he'd say that!" Kerry bursts out. "And I can't, I absolutely *can't*. She's never liked me and I don't like her."

Elaine's still on at McCasky.

"So what did *you* say?"

"I said if people knew he'd sent his daughter away, he could kiss goodbye to his business."

"You *what*? How d'you make that out?"

"I told him people on the island don't like that kind of thing, 'specially from a newcomer. I said they wouldn't deal with him if they heard what he'd done."

Elaine's eyebrows have gone up, and I know what she means. It's a rubbish story. People will gossip about Derek and say he's awful, but if they want what he sells they'll still buy it.

"Did he *believe* that?" she asks.

McCasky shrugs. "Why not? He's a stranger here. He just asked how they'd know."

He studies his beer can while he waits for us to think about it. He has great timing, I'll give him that. I can't resist feeding him the line.

"And how *would* they know?"

He smiles.

"I said I'd make damn sure they knew."

Kerry puts her hand over her mouth, then starts to giggle.

Elaine is doubled up with laughter.

"Fergus, you are wicked," she says.

She comes round the table and puts her hand on the back of his neck. "You know, that's what I missed." And she kisses him. I don't know where to look.

"You must go away more often," he says.

Then he goes into the sitting room and switches on the sports news.

Louise came to collect Kerry after we'd eaten. I didn't want to be downstairs on my own with McCasky and Elaine so I'm up here talking to Jess on the phone. I didn't much want to call her because of the way she broke her promise, but it had to be done some time.

"Well," she says after I've told her about Louise and Derek. "It's a good thing they know."

"Yeah," I say. "S'pose so."

There's another silence. This isn't going well.

"Look," she says, "I'm really sorry, Cal. I know I promised, but the more I thought about it, the more it seemed kind of – silly."

I'm not convinced.

"Anyway, it sounds as if Pop did a great job," she goes on. "And how about Kerry? How's she feeling?"

"Dunno, really. There have been other people around all the time. We haven't had a chance to talk."

"People don't have to be the enemy."

I'm not sure she's right. Some of them are OK, perhaps. Not many.

"Look, don't get depressed. Let's meet up when you see the tyres man next week, yeah?"

"I won't be seeing him. He's gone."

"What d'you mean, *gone*?"

"Got married, going to live in England. I'm supposed to see someone else. Some woman."

"Well, when you see her, then."

"I'm not going to."

"Oh, Cal. Come on."

"There's no point."

"What do you mean?"

Last night, I was awake for ages, thinking about what Miss Irvine had said. *People like us have to work very hard all the time at what we really want to do. It's the only way to be happy.* And I knew she was right. But things are all up in the air. It may turn out that I can't do what I really want, but I'll go for it while I can.

"Being on the mainland takes up a whole day," I tell Jess. "I'd miss a double music lesson."

She doesn't argue, just says, "It's great, the way you're sticking with music."

"Dunno. Pretty crazy, right now."

"No, it isn't."

There's a long pause. Then she amazes me.

"I should have done."

"Go on? You really mean, kept on with music?"

"Yeah. Made a bum choice. I thought I was doing the sensible thing, but the stuff at uni isn't creative like I'd hoped. And looking at what Caro's doing, interpreting data for hours every day – it's not for me."

This from the perfect Jess? An actual mistake? What a shame, though, if that's the way she really feels.

I ask, "Is it too late to change?"

"We're not far into the first term. I might be able to."

"Go for it."

"I think I will. Look, Cal, I can't talk any more just now, I've a practice with the guys."

"Have a good time," I say.

"Will do. You too. Thanks for hanging on to the music. You were right."

I never thought I'd hear her say anything like that.

Elaine lay awake beside the gently snoring bulk of Fergus, her face in the familiar hollow between his neck and shoulder. While undressing, she'd had a moment of thinking, *Kitty Reed took her clothes off in this bedroom.* But then, whose fault was that? Both she and Fergus had explored elsewhere. And tonight, the result had been highly enjoyable.

* * *

Elaine and I are in the Head's office.

"Most unfortunate," he's saying, fiddling with a pen between his fingers.

He won't look at me. I think he feels that sex is a club for married people with proper salaries.

He clears his throat and says, "I take it the girl concerned is not willing to consider a termination?"

"No," says Elaine.

"Has anyone spoken to her seriously about this? It really would be much the best option."

"It's the basic right of any woman to make that choice," Elaine says firmly. "You are right, of course, in all practical terms, but I absolutely can't try to persuade Kerry to do something she doesn't want to."

The Head glances at the clock on the wall. Elaine notices, of course.

"We are keeping you from more important things," she says.

"Not at all, not at all."

He's flustered, but he talks on.

"I take it Callum" – he risks a quick glance at me – "will continue at school and take his Highers? We have been pleased to see his improved attitude towards his work this term."

"Yes, he will," says Elaine. She stands up. "We will not trouble you any longer."

"Our pupil support adviser will be in touch with you."

He stands up and shakes hands with Elaine but not me, and we go out.

His troubles are not over. Kerry is coming along the corridor, with Derek and Louise. Louise smiles but Derek doesn't, just gives me a filthy look. Kerry and I touch hands as we pass, but we don't stop.

Best of luck, I think. But I'm not sure who needs it most, Kerry or the Head.

"Well," says the Goth, "this is going to be interesting, isn't it."

She seems dead chuffed. Anyone would think she was the baby's fairy godmother.

Kerry's sitting beside me in the pupil support office. I'd like to hold her hand, but we've got to look serious.

"There is the question of how to make it known," Mrs Mack goes on. "I don't think it's a good idea simply to leave people to notice. I wonder if we might just tell the people in your own year. What do you think?"

Kerry says, "I don't know."

Neither do I. It's going to be awful whatever way she does it.

"Right. Now, Kerry, you know you've a right to go on with your education, don't you? When you get to the later stages, we can arrange a home tutor."

She's probably done masses of training about youth

advising and never had any youth to advise. Now she's got us, and she's loving every minute.

I'm hating it. She's turning us into a "case".

I feel like I'm on show, like the ant colony on the internet, sandwiched between glass panels. You could see they were trying to get away into the dark, but there wasn't enough dark. They had to go up between the panels to get the food that was put in through a slot at the top. Their queen went on laying eggs because that's what she did, and the eggs were all pushed against the glass, too. She fertilized them from the sperm she'd kept in her pouch from the one and only time she mated. Or left them unfertilized, according to what the colony needed. She had no choice.

I have no choice.

Something awful's happening. My heart's thumping, I feel sick. I'm panicking. I'm going to scream. Mustn't scream, mustn't.

"You all right, Callum?" Mrs Mack asks.

I meant to say I'm fine but I haven't said it, I'm at the door, wrestling with the handle, push – no, pull.

Corridor, stairs, glass front doors. Push, yes right. Out.

Blue sky, clear as a glass sandwich.

Run, just run.

My lungs feel as if they're on fire. I'm well up the Forestry track now. I slow down. My legs are shaking. I lean against the nearest tree trunk, forehead against the rough bark. I put my palms on it. Slowly the rage and panic start to get less.

A sodding tree-hugger, McCasky would say.

He doesn't like tranquil faces and beatific smiles. What does he like? I don't know. Minutes go by.

I've started up the track again, walking now.

I didn't know I could get a girl pregnant.

Yes, I did, that's ridiculous. The sex education stuff made the mechanics of it perfectly clear. And I knew how animals did it. I even understood artificial insemination and why it was cheaper than keeping a bull. But I thought human sex was something to deal with later, when I was properly grown up, married perhaps. *Darling, shall we start a family?* It's not like that, of course. It isn't planned and conventional. Sex is the biggest thrill in the world, all the closeness and excitement you could ever hope for. It's like you're cuddled and loved as if you were a baby again, perfect and adored, and at the same time you have all this power. But it comes back and hits you.

If we could be together in the way we dreamed of, it would be fine – but we can't. Everything's changed, it's all spoiled. Even the bothy. It's turning into a building site. McCasky's sent a couple of men up to put new timbers on the roof and make it waterproof. He's like one of his own mechanical diggers, barging on, getting things done. I wonder why he got that way. It's a shame you can't know your parents before they had you. He might have had some dream that he gave up when he settled for being a builder. But he'd never say so. Just listens to Dolly Parton and Cat Stevens, and hums along.

I've come to the top of the hill, where the track goes on across to the other side of the island. I can go that way, then circle down towards Kilkeddie. It's a lot further, but I'm in no hurry. Kerry will still be in school, she won't get to the bothy until later. It's almost autumn, but the sun is high above the hill's edge. It's very hot. I take my school shirt off and tie it round my waist. The tie is already stuffed into my pocket.

Walking is good. It's a basic rhythm, like a heartbeat. Shut in school, you lose touch with that. It's all scraps of broken direction and none of it hangs together properly, and you start to feel frantic. At least, I do. Maybe it's OK for the others, but I can't imagine being anyone else, I'm stuck with being me.

I'm coming to the first trees. Two Scots pines, up here on their own. Very tall, very old and strong. There's a smooth rock beside one of them and I sit down and lean my arms on my knees, the way I did that day on the bench above our house, before I'd met Kerry. The heat of it under my legs in their school trousers is only just bearable.

The Goth still thinks I'm aiming to do dentistry. But I'd have to spend my life in a small room with blinds at the windows, looking into the mouths of patient after patient even if they're stupid and smell awful. I just can't.

An ant runs over my foot. Even up here, there are ants. Doing what they have to do. They cause no harm. I lean my head back against the tree and let my hands drop. Tears come from my closed eyes, but they are somehow tears of relief.

It's got to be music.

I can't do anything else. It probably won't make money or anything, but music is what I am. My carrier wave, my rhythm. It's the only thing that connects me with other humans. Kerry and I – it's like we're in the same key. Singing the same song with different notes and different words.

The decision stands there like the sun in the sky. The Goth won't like it. Neither will the Head. But they can get on with running their processing machine. Count me out.

"Oh, no," said Elaine, phone to her ear. "When did he go?"

"He walked out of a one-to-one session with him and Kerry first period this afternoon," said Mrs Mack. "I hoped he'd be back by the end of the session. But he isn't. I've just checked that he's not on the Kilkeddie bus. There's probably no cause for alarm, but I thought I should let you know."

"Yes. Thank you."

Elaine's mind was racing. *Someone fell down the cliff above the waterfall three years ago, and it was 48 hours before they found her. No, surely he wouldn't do that.*

"Was the session going all right?" she asked. "He didn't seem stressed or anything?"

"It was fine," said Mrs Mack. "We were discussing the best way to break the news of the pregnancy to the other pupils, then I mentioned the possibility of a home tutor for Kerry. He started to look agitated, then he just got up and bolted out. Kerry suggested he might have needed the toilet. She's quite a practical girl."

"Yes," Elaine said again.

Practical. I must be practical.

"I'd better get off the phone in case he tries to call me," she said. "I'll let you know the minute I have any news."

"Good. I'll give you my mobile number in case it's after school hours."

Elaine wrote it down.

"Thank you so much," she said again. In her experience, people always wanted lots of thanks.

"It's the least I could do," said Mrs Mack. Then she added, "I'm just glad you're there."

Meaning, I haven't been. What a dreadful mother, leaving my family. No wonder things like this happen.

Elaine hung up and went outside.

The heat of the day was ebbing. Autumn was on its way. The rowan berries were starting to turn red. The sun was only just above the hill's edge.

Callum's out there somewhere. What's happened? Has it all become too much for him?

Fear churned in her stomach.

She went across to the office.

"Sorry to bother you," she said as the usual silence fell. "Is Fergus about?"

"He's at the Blackwood site," said Maggie Lawson, and turned back to her screen.

Elaine went back into the house and called Fergus but got his voicemail.

"Callum's walked out of school," she said. "Nobody knows where he is. There's nothing much we can do, but I just thought I'd tell you."

Anything to add? Not really.

"See you later. Bye."

Mrs Ambrose would be here at any minute. She would want to talk about her bunions, and whether they could be massaged away. Silly idea, but she was scared of surgery.

Elaine stared out of the window again. *If she's scared, she's scared. Same as I am, right now. Dear God – please take care of my son.* It was a long time since she'd prayed, and she felt faintly embarrassed. She must not sound as if she took the Almighty for granted. *If it be Thy will. Amen.*

It would be so wonderful, she thought, to have real faith.

Chapter 18

There's still some gas in the cylinder. Put the kettle on.

I sit down on the bench. I'm a lot later than I meant. Shouldn't have gone the longer way, I got lost a bit and it took ages. It's dark in here with the roofing felt on properly, and the place has the sharp smell of new timber. There's a saw-bench in the middle of the floor with a tarpaulin over it. Some light still comes in through the doorway, but it's dim and cool in here. I button my shirt up. The leaves on the elder tree outside are turning yellow. Everything's changing, things are not the way they were. It could have been so good, living here.

No, it couldn't. Let's face it, the bothy was a ruin. It still is. McCasky is licking it into shape, but it'll be next year before we start coming up here again – if we ever do. We were playing at being grown up then it went real, like a kitten turns into a cat. The dream isn't there any more.

With the baby coming, Kerry's going to need proper care.

The kettle whistles. I get up, put a teabag in a mug, pour the water on. And Kerry's at the door.

She doesn't come in.

She says, "I'll go away if you want."

"*Go away*? What do you mean?"

"You ran out. If it's because of me, you'd better say."

"Because of *you*? You can't think—"

"Yes, I can."

She's angry. Seriously angry. She takes a step forward and words start pouring out.

"We were talking to Mrs Mack about what we have to do. It was quite important stuff, but you got up and walked out. OK. If you can't face the idea of sticking around, that's fine, I'll manage on my own. But you've got to tell me."

I'm scared she'll go away and never come back, and I'll be more alone than I've ever been in my life.

"It *wasn't* because of you."

"Well, it looked to me like it was. And Mrs Mack, too. She thought it was weird. We both waited for you to come back. But you didn't."

We, she says. She's lined up with the Goth against me. Can't argue, though. She's right.

"I'm really sorry."

She takes no notice.

"If you don't want to go on, you've got to say. I'd rather know now."

"Of *course* I want to go on."

I move towards Kerry very carefully, like she's a wild deer or something, because I'm scared she'll turn and run. But she doesn't move.

"Well," she says huskily, "that's good."

And the next minute I'm holding her close. We haven't been alone together for ages, the days have been cluttered up with other people. If we were different, if we'd belonged to stuffy, conventional families and said the words that make us married, we wouldn't be standing here in a half-mended ruin as the darkness comes. We'd have a warm bed to look forward to, and a right to share it.

After a bit she says, "Your tea's getting cold."

I make tea for her as well, and we sit down on the bench. I put my arm round her again. I never want to let her go.

She says, "Where have you been?"

"I was just – walking."

"Where did you go?"

"I'm not sure. Got a bit lost."

I try to take a sip of tea but my hair gets in my mouth so I shift my arm from round Kerry so as to push it back. Nuisance. I'm asking the question almost before I mean to.

"Do we have any scissors?"

"In the tool box," Kerry says. "They're not much good. Why?"

"Can you cut my hair?"

"Like – *now*?"

"Yeah. I'm fed up with it."

"You mean, really short?"

"Dunno. What do you think?"

She looks at me carefully.

"Could be OK. Shame, though. I like it long."

"I used to. But I'm sick of it."

She gets up and rakes around our plastic tray of tools, and comes back with a big pair of scissors with chipped blue paint on the handles.

"These are crap," she says.

"Don't care."

She drapes one of our old rugs round my shoulders. I hold its edges together under my chin.

"You sure about this?"

"Yep. Go for it."

"OK."

She starts holding long bits up and sawing them off. The scissors sound like a dog chewing.

"You're going blond at the roots," she says.

"Gave up bothering."

"Ah, c'mon. Orange is great."

It's nice that she still cares. She goes on hacking away with the blunt scissors.

"I reckon that's it," she says at last. "If I do any more it'll just look worse."

She gathers the rug from my shoulders and stands

back, holding it. And laughs.

"You look weird. But it's the best I can do."

I push my hands through what's left of it while Kerry shakes the rug out of the door. It feels like there's nothing left. I hadn't meant it to be that short. Too late now, though. I stand up and bend over, shaking my head. There's a huge amount of orange hair on the floor. Kerry's fetched the broom from the corner.

"Mind," she says. She starts sweeping it up.

It's getting dark. We shouldn't have done the haircut right now – Elaine will be in a panic. She may have notified the Mountain Rescue squad. Oh hell. This was stupid.

"We'd better get back."

Kerry doesn't argue.

"Come on, then."

"Callum! Oh, thank goodness!"

Elaine jumps up from where she was sitting at the kitchen table and runs into the hall. "Fergus, they're here!"

Then she comes back.

"We've been so worried. The school rang to say you'd walked out, and everyone's been notified – police and everything. They said it wasn't urgent yet, but they'll need to know you're safe. Where did you *go*? And what on earth have you done to your hair? Don't tell me you ducked out of school to get it styled?"

"*Styled*," murmurs Kerry. "Wow."

McCasky comes in. He just stands there, looking.

"Sorry," I say.

He asks Elaine, "Have you let the school know?"

"They've just this minute come in. I'll call Mrs Mack."

She picks up the phone and starts tapping in the number.

"I don't know where you've been," McCasky says to me, "and I don't want to know. But you have a mobile. You could have used it."

"I couldn't get a signal."

But I never tried, and he probably knows it.

"Your mother's been worried sick. That mean anything to you?"

"Yes. I really am sorry."

"Don't do it again. Ever."

"I won't."

It's amazing he's not shouting.

Elaine's got through to Mrs Mack.

"No, I don't have any details yet, they've only just come in," she's saying, "but I thought I'd better—"

McCasky hasn't finished.

"When Elaine's off the phone, you will call the Mountain Rescue yourself, and explain what you were doing. And then the police. Right?"

"Right."

Oh, God. But I suppose I deserve it.

McCasky turns to Kerry.

"You'd better phone your family and tell them where you are. If you need a lift home, let me know."

He goes back to his television. There's a roar of applause from the other room, as if he'd earned it. Goal.

Part 3
Chapter 19

November, and it's chucking it down with rain. We're upstairs in my room. I'm playing my guitar and Kerry's standing by the window with her hands on the radiator, staring out at the grey garden. She comes back with me from school most days, unless her mum needs her to look after the boys.

Elaine's always bringing us cups of tea and stuff. I know she means well, but it kind of rubs it in that we don't have a place of our own. We're being looked after and fed as if we were still children. I ought to be grateful. At least we didn't get chucked out. We could be in some grim hostel or sleeping in shop doorways.

But we don't have a life of our own. Kerry goes back to her mother's house every night. The single bed in here stays single. It's the one I've had since I was a kid. We're not a couple. It gives me this feeling our families think this is just a mistake that'll get tidied up; a patch of trouble that'll blow over if you don't take too much notice. Like the horrible Danes going on eating their pastries while the dolphins get butchered.

To be fair, it was Elaine who showed me the e-mail about the dolphins. She said afterwards she wished she hadn't, because she thought it had upset me, but she signed the petition. I don't suppose McCasky did.

I'm not so scared of him now. I'm still kind of careful, but he's different. Maybe Elaine going off to Greece gave him a fright, even though he moved Kitty in like he just needed a housekeeper. It wasn't just that, though. Let's face it, he was sleeping with her. But then, he probably knew Elaine hadn't gone to Greece on her own – I can see that now. So he could think, *Anything my wife does, I can do, too.* Could be he was more upset than he let on. I don't know. He'd never tell anyone. Perhaps he's just a bit more careful now, same as I am.

There's such a lot I don't know. In April, Kerry and I will be parents. We ought to be doing something about it, not just sitting up here while it rains outside.

McCasky's done nothing more to the bothy. At least the place won't fall down any further, and it's watertight. He put a door on it, with a lock. He said I could have the key if I wanted, but there's no point. We can't live there.

I don't know what we can do. Nobody's saying anything about the future. It's all a big silence. Maybe Elaine assumes she'll look after the baby while Kerry and I go on at school, same as before. I can't see Kerry doing that. She's gone kind of quiet, though. I don't know what she's thinking. The last few days, she's seemed really down.

She's still standing there at the window, staring at nothing much. I lay my guitar on the bed and ask, "You OK?"

She doesn't answer at first, and when she does, she's still looking out at the rain.

"Is it going to be like this all winter?"

"Can't tell, really."

Must try to cheer her up.

"We get bright days," I say. "It's nice when it snows. Blue sky and the hills all white."

"It's summer in Australia."

She leans her forehead on the glass. I go over to her. She's crying. Not making any sound, just tears trickling down her face.

"Hey – sweetheart. What is it?"

I put my arm round her and she turns to me with a sigh, as if she's very tired.

"I'm so homesick."

"For Australia?"

She nods.

"Why?"

"The sun. Every morning, you get up and it's hot. I just – want to be there."

She rubs her eyes on the back of her hand.

"Sorry," she says. "Not your fault."

"It is. Well, kind of."

"Nah. I chose to come here. I could have left school and stayed on. Got a job of some sort. But Neil and Micky would have been upset. I looked after them a lot when Mum was busy with the horses. They'd have missed me."

"I thought you liked it here."

"It was OK in the summer. But it's so cold now, and wet. And dark. I feel like I'm in prison."

"Ah, c'mon."

How can she say that? It's so easy to be out on the hill, and you can see for miles up there, the sea lying below you, mainland away on the horizon. But I suppose it's different for Kerry. She didn't grow up here, she's not been used to that. She was free to be out on her own here, no problem – at least, until Derek found out about the baby – but she always said the place was "kinda small".

She picks up my thoughts as if I'd spoken.

"Back home, there's so much space," she says. "It goes on and on."

I know what she means. It's in the music she sings. The people she comes from have been there for thousands of years. They understand how it works – at least, they used to, before the white invaders took over. I didn't get any of that at first, until I looked it up on the internet. The things the colonials did to the Kooris were unbelievable. The pictures of the outback are scary, though. So huge and red and empty. Just waiting to kill you. Hugeness can be a prison, too.

"I've got to go back," she says.

My heart almost stops.

"Back to *Australia*? But you *can't*. I mean…"

"Not right now. I'll have to stay until the baby's born. I'll go soon after, though. It'll be easier while it's small enough to carry. You can get those liddle back-pack things."

She's got it all planned. And the plan is just for her and the baby. The hurt of it thumps me in the gut.

"So where do I come in? Or don't I?"

She looks at me very straight.

"If you want to come with me, that would be great. But I couldn't plan for that, could I? You might not want to. It's best to expect the worst. That way, if it turns out to be tough, at least you're not surprised. Anything better – well, that's a bonus."

I'll never understand her, but there's one thing for sure. She's not going anywhere without me.

"I'm coming with you," I say. "I don't care where it is."

Her face brightens. "Go on? I didn't think you would."

"Why?"

She shrugs.

"Don't take this wrong, Cal."

She pauses, then goes on.

"You've always had things easy. I know you worry about stuff, but you talk about going to university like it's just something you choose. Or don't choose, if that suits you better. You might be a dentist. Or it's music. Fine. Either way, you'll be off to college, take it for granted."

"But—"

She's not stopping.

"I mucked about in school before I came here. Never bothered learning anything. College? Forget it. They must have thought I was a total pain in the arse."

"Same as me."

"It's *not* the same. You stopped working because of worrying about the world and not wanting to be a human. Your trouble is, you get ideas like other people get HIV."

"That's not fair."

But she's not stopping.

"With you it's all dreamtime. That's OK, it's what men do, it's what makes them into explorers and artists, it's a kind of system. The Kooris dream their way across thousands of miles of Australia because it's like music to them, they know its tunes. At least, the men do. But the women don't sing those songs, they've got kids to look after, food to find and cook. Those things are a must. Men don't have to split in half to make a new person that's gonna go on being part of them, they're free."

She stops. She thumps her head as if she's realized something.

"Jeez. That's it, isn't it? That's the prison. It's not the island, it's the baby. Why didn't I see?"

And there was me thinking how great it must be.

"I'd love to be that close," I tell her. "I'm not connected

to the baby like you are, I'm outside. I don't matter in the same way. I never will. I envy you."

She stares at me.

"I didn't know you felt like that."

"It's not what I *think*. I mean, we ought to be trying to cut down the number of humans. But yeah, it's what I feel."

I'm not like Jess. She's taking good care to stay free. Maybe females come in different kinds. Like, mothers and others.

"Kerry," I ask, "did you always want a baby? I mean, before you met me?"

She thinks about it.

"Dunno. Yeah, maybe I did. From when I was small, if I thought about being grown up, it was always with kids around."

She makes a rueful face.

"Guess I *wanted* to split in half. But I didn't know that. When I got older I just felt very sexy. But then – what's sex *for*?"

"Reproduction of the species."

And where does that leave me? Standing in a field like some bull or tup, job done? Or like the successful one out of the useless hundreds of drone ants? How stupid can you get?

"Cal."

She pushes her fingers through my scruffy short hair, making me look at her.

"Listen. I don't just love you – I *like* you. I like being with you, looking at you, talking to you, doing music. I want us to be together. But only if that's what you want, too. If you don't, it's OK. I'd be dead sad, but me and the baby, we can go back where I came from, and you'll be free to get on with your life."

She must be joking. Stupid or not, I'm not having that.

"Sorry," I tell her. "You're going to have to count me in."

Her arms are round my neck.

She kisses me.

I need her in the same way that she needs the huge sun of Australia.

McCasky is flipping through the post. He chucks most of it on the table unopened but he rips open a white envelope, reads the letter it contains then tosses it on the table with a nod of satisfaction.

"Planning permission granted for the bothy," he says. "Subject to agreement from the Forestry for improvement of the access track."

What? I didn't know he'd even applied for planning permission. Elaine's looking startled, too.

"You mean, you really think it would make a house?" she asks.

McCasky doesn't bother with the question.

"I don't want to lay the men off if work's short. The bothy's a useful thing to have on the side."

"It's very small," Elaine objects. "And there's no space round it, the hill's too close."

"It'll do as a starter home," he says. "Or a holiday let if that falls through."

He glances at me and I put my hand to my mouth, but Elaine still doesn't get it.

"There's no sea view or anything," she says. "It might be better to offer it to the Housing Association. They've so many people on their list. A young couple—"

"Quite," says McCasky.

At last Elaine clocks. Her face flushes because she's been so silly – and because she's pleased.

"Oh, Fergus, that's lovely! What a brilliant idea!"

"If it doesn't work out I can sell it," he says.

Which is pretty brave, the way the housing market is right now. I ought to get up and hug him or something, but I can't go that far. So I just say, "Thanks."

He gives me a nod.

But we may never live in the bothy. Could be we're trekking across Australia, Kerry and me and the baby. I can't tell him that. I can't tell anyone.

Perhaps it won't happen. But I want it to.

At least, I think I do.

Jess is home for a weekend. She and Kerry and I have come up to the waterfall. It's the first week of December, and we've had snow. It didn't last long at sea level, but up here everything is still white. And the waterfall is frozen. Kerry's staring at it in astonishment. The cold has blasted it into droopy white shapes like some crazy ice-sculptor has been at work, and the water that usually slides down over the rock face has set solid. The dark pool far below is probably solid as well – though it may not be. It's very deep. A girl fell over the edge of the waterfall once. They didn't find her for two days.

"That is stunning," Kerry says.

She starts taking photos, mooching about in the snow to find the best angle.

"It's good to be out of the city," Jess says.

"I thought you liked Glasgow."

"Well, yeah, I do. But I need this as well. I didn't realize how much."

She brushes the snow off the wooden rail that fences off the drop and leans her arms on it.

"School or college, you're so busy, you don't know how much there is out there," she says. "What a lot of stuff you've never thought of. It's like you've been a battery chicken."

"Is it better now you're back to music?"

"Yeah. Bit of luck, someone dropping out of the synthesis course because it was too difficult. Electronics and composition go perfectly."

"Great," I say.

Lucky old Jess, found the game she's meant for. Like it

said in the *Just So* story. *Payah kun. Quite right.* But I guess you can't find it on purpose, it just has to happen.

"I'm into communication, you see," Jess says. "I didn't get the idea at school, but I can see it now. Music's communication, same as technology is. It came first, maybe even before we had words. Kerry's Aboriginal stuff – it's so ancient it gives me the shivers. Remember that day I came back to school and I heard her sing? That's when I knew I'd picked the wrong thing."

Kerry comes to join us, pushing her camera into her pocket.

Jess says, "I was just telling Cal, I was knocked out by your singing. It started me on a whole new thing."

"Go on?" says Kerry. "Really?" She looks pleased.

"Very much really," Jess says. "I've shifted the course I was doing at uni. I expect Cal told you. I'm desperate to find out more about Aboriginal music."

Kerry says, "I want to know more, too." She gives me a glance. "That's one of the reasons I've got to go back."

I haven't told Jess about the Australia idea. She looks at me in astonishment.

"New thing," I say. "I'm still trying to get my head round it."

Jess never takes long to grab a new idea.

"That is terrific," she says, and turns back to Kerry. "When will you go?"

"Dunno. Not till after the baby's born."

"Could be brilliant. I'm being dead selfish, but if you and Cal are actually *there*..."

Then she looks back at me.

"Is that the plan?"

"Yeah," says Kerry. "That's the plan."

Jess rushes on.

"I'd been thinking I'd have to research it on the internet and maybe ask your advice," she says. "But if I could come over and actually be there – oh, wow. I could hang on a bit and do a doctorate or something. But I need to get some basics now."

Kerry's not listening. She's staring at the waterfall again, but thinking of something else. I know now why she wants to go back. It's not just the heat of the sun. It's the people she came from. Her father, who went away into the hot emptiness of Australia and stayed there.

Suddenly she smiles and puts both hands on the front of her coat, looking down.

"Hey," she said. "It just moved."

"Well, hello, baby," Jess says.

We stand there, the three of us. Four, if you count the little one that's just woken up. We're smiling like idiots. Our breath steams in the cold air.

Chapter 20

The snow went on a long time. It thawed after Christmas then the sky turned dark again and dumped another lot on us. January, February... It's the end of March now, and people are sick of snow, 'specially the ones who live up the tracks. They've been trudging across fields, welly-boot-deep in the stuff, to get to the main road and the bus. But now green shoots of daffodils are coming up, and snowdrops are blooming in sheltered places, a different whiteness, fresh and bright.

I'm at the bothy. It's Sunday afternoon, so the men aren't here. They've put a septic tank in, and the foundations have been cemented where they're going to build a bathroom out the back. Kerry said she felt too knackered to go anywhere.

I don't think she really likes the bothy now. She fronted up to McCasky last week and said, "It's great what you're doing. But – we didn't ask."

He said, "No, you didn't," and went outside to get another bit of timber.

End of conversation.

She wears baggy sweaters bought from the charity shop over trousers with leggings underneath because of the cold. She doesn't look that big. Some of the girls at school are bulkier than she is, even though they're not having babies.

The home tutor thing started last term, so she doesn't come to school any more. Elaine said she was welcome to do the sessions at our place, but Derek said Kerry was his daughter and the tutor would come to his house. Kerry says her mum's got masses of baby clothes together. So has Elaine. Now the news is out, people keep giving her things. Nobody has said what's going to happen after the baby is born.

It's very cold in here, and it smells of sawn timber. It isn't our secret place any more, it's a building site. Stupid to regret that – it's what we dreamed of, turning the bothy into a proper house. McCasky is doing a great job. I just hope he's not expecting us to live in it, happy ever after. It's all too uncertain for that. I haven't told him or Elaine about Australia, and Jess swears she won't.

"Honest," she says. "I'm keeping out of it."

Maybe Kerry will change her mind when the baby comes.

There's nothing much I can do here. I take the broom from where it stands in the corner and sweep up the wood shavings on the new floor. Underneath it, the ants will be lying doggo for the winter. Or ant-o. Using the stores they laid down in the summer, conserving energy.

Jess still thinks ants are the perfect super-computer, but last time we talked about it, we got onto the question of who would be in charge. Computers need a user. The big idea, of course, is to make one that doesn't need a user, but it's hard to get the head round that. That's where ants come in. They don't have a user. They make their own queen and she doesn't have any choice about how she behaves because she is part of the ant-brain, so what they do goes round and round on its own. But who programmed that? God? Evolution? Can you separate evolution from God? I don't know, it's too big to think of.

Humans are peculiar. We're besotted with the idea of being in charge. We'd like to be God, but only so we can grab as much as we can. When we've finished, there'll be nothing left, but we don't even care. It's like our collective brain-machine doesn't have a user, unless it's God. And if God let all this start, he, she or it will sit back and watch it run down and stop.

Nothing to be done.

I stand the broom back in the corner then go out and pull the new door shut behind me.

Elaine was digging over a bed near the top of the garden. March. Time to put in broad beans. She should have sown them last autumn for an early crop, but the garden hadn't been the main thing on her mind at that time.

Her mind was full of the coming baby, though there were four weeks to go. *Poor wee mite. It's going to be born to hopeless parents.* The thought made her feel guilty, but she defended it. Callum was no more than a troubled boy, and Kerry came from strange, wandering stock. She had refused to have a scan, so they didn't know the sex of the baby. She said it would be all right or it wouldn't, and she wasn't going to change anything anyway.

She's very attractive. Lots of energy and charm. Practical, too, and willing. The perfect daughter-in-law. Or daughter-out-of-law.

But the fact remained, Kerry had enchanted Callum and changed him from a child to a baffled and unready father. He was responsible, of course, there was no ducking that – but accepting responsibility for a woman and a child was a lot to ask of someone only just seventeen.

Louise, the baby's other grandmother, seemed a nice woman, if a bit harassed. She had come round with some more baby stuff yesterday, and stayed for a coffee. She said Kerry wanted to go back to Australia, but it was unlikely to come to anything. The poor girl probably had that trapped feeling that comes in late pregnancy. And Callum wouldn't want to go traipsing off to the other side of the world – he had his education to think of.

Really, there's only me, Elaine thought. And Fergus. *He's*

been amazingly good about it. But I must be careful not to be
pushy. Callum needs help, but he likes to think he doesn't.

She had heard nothing from Andrew after a single letter filled with polite regret. Patsy told her he'd taken the Paris job and was living happily in a flat above a cafe in the Rue de Bac. She hadn't said whether he'd found someone else.

Australia.

Elaine lifted another forkful of earth, broke it and pulled out a dandelion.

Once she's had the baby she'll feel different.

We're doing an end-of-term concert, proceeds to go to the Haiti Earthquake appeal. Miss Irvine asked if we could get *Sign On* together. Jess couldn't make it, but there's a clarinet girl who's pretty good, so we're on the stage, hammering into a fast version of "Hit the Road, Jack". We're the last item on the programme except for the final sing-along. Star billing. Some of the girls are dancing in the space in front of the first row of seats, really going for it. I can see the Head in the front row, looking pained. He probably likes Cliff Richard.

We bring it to an end and the place goes mad, yelling and shouting, stamping their feet. It's like the concert last summer when Kerry came up, all excited, only more so.

I hadn't properly met Kerry then. I keep thinking I'll see her pushing through the audience, same as she did then.

But I won't. She's in hospital on the mainland. The baby isn't due until next week, but anyone having a first baby has to be in well before the date. Otherwise, if anything goes wrong, it's a radio call for the helicopter, blue lights flashing on the playing field where it lands, paramedics in high-viz jackets. Choppering people off is expensive and I suppose Kerry's safer where she is. She's dead bored, though. I've been phoning her every day but there isn't much to talk about. I haven't been able to go over to see her because of school.

We shift the gear back to clear the stage and the senior girls' choir gets into place. They all adore Miss Irvine so there are dozens of them. They plunge into "Will Ye No' Come Back Again" and the audience joins in.

I check my phone. There's a text.

hi cal ive started. b ok dont worry xxxxx k

Oh, my God.

I feel hot and cold all over. I want to be there. But there's no boat until tomorrow.

I text back, *wish I was there. b with u tmrw xxxxxxxxxxxxx c*

The choir has shifted into "Loch Lomond".

I go out back-stage and stand in the empty corridor, wishing I wasn't here. People are coming out of the gym, down the far end, with rolled up mats and rugs. Yoga class. Not the sort who go to loud concerts.

I go into the toilet, to avoid meeting them. I feel as if I'm walking in a bad dream. There's my face in the mirror, same as always. My ratty-looking hair is streaky pale, the orange is growing out. Kerry wanted me to dye it again but I couldn't be bothered. I'll do it, though, if she wants me to. I have a pee and wash my hands slowly.

The notice above the basins says, CAUTION, WATER MAY BE VERY HOT.

CAUTION, LIFE MAY BE VERY HOT.

Too late for caution.

I've made another person. Added to the curse of the planet. And I'm not even properly sorry, I'm just dead scared it may kill Kerry.

You get ideas like other people get HIV, she said.

But you can't die of ideas, I tell her.

Yes, you can. What if you get blown up by a terrorist?

That's because someone turned an idea into something real.

Why has my brain gone running off like a dog after a stick?

It's just, I want to talk to her and I can't.

And she's in danger.

I feel sick. Why didn't I think what I was doing?

Because it's not about thinking, it's because you're only an ant and you're not equipped to think, you just do as...

I can't stop the torrent of words that are raging in my head. I don't know what they're about, and I don't care. I just want to be with her.

Liam comes in. I don't know how long I've been

standing here with my hands on the edge of the basin. There's a babble of noise from the hall, people coming out.

"You all right?" he says.

"Yeah."

I turn away and put my hands under the hot-air dryer, though they've dried on their own. I can feel him looking at me.

"How's Kerry?" he asks.

It's a six-count before I can answer.

"She's started having it. She texted me."

"Wow. Awesome."

No words come.

He gives my shoulder a gentle shake.

"C'mon," he says. "She'll be OK."

"Sure."

But nothing's sure.

Liam says, "Your mum and dad are outside. You'd better come and see them."

He herds me out in front of him, like I'm a sheep.

I'm going to have to tell them.

Baa-aaa.

Dawn. The red sun is making a gash between the heavy clouds over the sea. I didn't mean to wake this early. I put on the light and check my mobile. No messages. Can't call her phone, she might be…

I hit the ward number she gave me.

A woman answers.

"Maternity."

"Oh, hi. It's – um – I'm Cal McCasky. I wondered how Kerry is. Kerry Donovan."

"Are you a relative?"

I don't know what she means.

"No. I mean, I'm not her brother or anything."

"I'm sorry, we can only give information to relatives."

Click.

God's sake.

I try again. Same voice.

"Hi. I spoke to you just now. Thing is, I'm Kerry's – I mean, I'm the baby's father."

She sounds cross.

"Well then, you are a relative, aren't you? Yes, they're both fine. You can come in later. Visiting is two to four, six-thirty to eight."

"When was it born?"

"Three forty-five this morning. A boy."

Click.

A *boy*.

Kerry's made a male child, same kind as me. It doesn't seem real. I ought to feel different. I don't know how I feel. Just, I must be dreaming.

Outside, the red streak between the clouds has got wider. The sky above them is glowing pink all the way up into the last of the dark. I don't know what to do. No point in going for the first boat, I'd be hanging around all morning before they let me in. I can't phone Kerry yet. It's not long since she had the baby, and I don't know how she'll be. Everyone says it hurts like hell.

I'll never know.

I get back into bed. My feet are freezing. I put the light out and pull the duvet up over my ears.

Chapter 21

Bill's in the queue at the cafeteria counter on the boat.

"All right, are you?" he says.

He smiles a lot now. His new teeth look too big for his face, but he's dead pleased with them.

"Fine," I say.

I'm not telling Bill. Not telling anyone yet. It was bad enough telling Elaine.

"I'm going for a fitting," he tells me. "I had these ones in straight away but they make you a better set later. Best thing I ever did," he adds. "Wish I'd gone for it years ago. Bacon roll, please," he tells the guy who's dishing out the food, and flashes a smile at him, too.

I go on past the food bit and get a mug of coffee. I take it upstairs to a corner of the non-observation lounge, hoping Bill won't find me. I don't feel like the ongoing denture saga this morning.

Elaine wanted to come with me but McCasky said, "It's

his kid, not yours. You can go later."

She looked so disappointed, I nearly gave in, but she said, "Well, all right, then. And actually, I do have a client."

"There you go, then," McCasky said.

I kind of miss hating him. Maybe it was just a habit.

The maternity department is very warm. The air feels like a woolly blanket.

A nurse says, "Through those doors, dear, third room on the right."

The doors have circular windows at face height and they swing both ways. They open into a corridor with notices on the walls about eating fresh fruit and how bad it is to smoke. There are rooms on both sides. I pass the first door on the right, then the second. I put my hand out to the third one – and it's opened from inside. A big bloke in a high-visibility jacket and work boots almost falls over me because he's looking back.

"Bye, love, see you this evening," he says. "Oh, sorry, son. Come to see your mum, have you?"

Talk about embarrassing.

There are four beds but somehow I can't look properly, my mind is jumping about. The woman in the nearest one is still smiling at the door where the work boots man is doing a last wave through the window. A blonde woman in the next bed is reading a magazine. She glances up without interest then goes on reading. The bed against the opposite wall is stripped and empty. Someone is huddled down under the bedclothes in the other one. I'm scared I'm in the wrong place.

"You looking for Kerry, dear?" asks the woman who was waving.

"Yes."

"That's her, over there. Having a wee sleep."

My trainers squeak on the polished floor though I'm trying to walk quietly. I can only see the top of her head. Her hand is curled over her face. I don't want to wake her.

There's a plastic cot beside the bed.

The baby is lying on his back with his fists resting beside his ears. He's dark, like Kerry. A brown baby. He's got soft black hair. His eyes are closed and he looks completely calm and peaceful. I put my hand out to touch him, then take it back. Perhaps I shouldn't.

Kerry's awake.

"Hi," she says.

She's smiling. I sit on the edge of the bed and lean down to kiss her.

"Isn't he beautiful?" she says.

"Yes, he is. You're wonderful. Making him."

"It took both of us," she says. "He's yours, too."

If we were somewhere else, I'd get into bed beside her and put my arms round her, carefully so as not to hurt her – but this is a hospital. I'm not sure if I'm even allowed to sit on the bed, but blow that.

The baby gives a little spluttering noise. I'm terrified.

"Is he all right?"

"He's fine," Kerry says.

How does she know? But she does.

"Do you want to pick him up?" she asks.

"Can I?"

"Sure. Put your hand under his head, he can't hold it up on his own yet."

I gather the baby up, together with the white blanket that's covering him, cradling his head as Kerry told me. He's heavier than I'd expected. He feels kind of solid and very warm, packed with everything that's going to grow bigger with him. His face is concentrated, like he's trying hard to understand this new state of being outside, with air all round him.

The feel of his head in my hand brings back the first moment when I saw Kerry on the boat, when I wanted to run my hand through her hair and feel the warmth of her skull underneath. Weird. That want has led straight to this.

The baby frowns and opens his mouth in a yawn. He starts to cry. It's surprisingly loud.

"He's probably hungry," Kerry says. "I don't have proper milk yet, but he needs the colostrum – that's what comes first."

She hitches herself up in the bed and unbuttons the bleached-looking hospital gown she's wearing, then holds her arms out. Very carefully, I hand the baby over. She puts him to her breast. He latches on at once and starts to suck greedily. Kerry arches her back and gives a little gasp. I'm scared all over again.

"What is it?"

"Sucking gives you a contraction, like when you're in labour," she says. "It hurts a bit but it's good, it helps get things back in the right place."

"How do you know so much about it?"

"I was around when my brothers were born. Mum said she hated being in hospital when she had me, so she insisted on home births after that. People thought she was mad."

I watch the baby sucking. It's a bit strange. When we made love, I used to do what he's doing now, not for milk but because it was all part of the most exciting thing I'd ever discovered. And it was just sex, using me to make a new human.

The really weird thing is, I don't mind. All I want right now is for the baby to finish feeding so I can hold him again and feel his small strength waiting to grow.

A new thought comes. It's one we haven't talked about, Kerry always said, "Wait and see first." Like it might be unlucky. But I can ask now.

"What are we going to call him?"

"Bardo," says Kerry.

I try it out.

"Bardo."

Yes. Sounds good.

"What does it mean?"

"Water. He was made on an island, so it's right for him."

"Yes."

But what about his other name? I'm sure she's going to say it'll be hers. Better get used to saying it.

"Bardo Donovan?"

She shakes her head.

"Donovan isn't my right name," she says. "I don't even know what my real name is, but it doesn't matter. He's Bardo McCasky."

Bardo McCasky.

It sounds wonderful. I'm smiling all over my face, like Bill on the boat. Like the man who met me at the door. I'm the same as him. I'm a father.

"Herbal?" Elaine offered.

Patsy nodded. "Something pink," she said.

"Raspberry and echinacea?"

"Perfect."

Patsy sighed luxuriously, leaning back against her chair in the kitchen.

"I always feel great after a session with you. So relaxed."

"That's good."

Elaine poured on the steaming water and watched it turn a deep red in the two mugs. After she and Andrew had parted, she hadn't much wanted to keep Patsy on as a client. But Patsy had protested that whatever her brother had done, it wasn't her fault, and that was fair enough.

"Teabag out or in?"

"In," said Patsy. "I like all the flavour I can get."

After a sip, she asked, "How's Kerry? Any news from the hospital yet?"

Elaine put her mug carefully on the table. Then she said, "The baby was born early this morning. It's a boy. They're both fine. Cal's gone to see her."

He wouldn't let me come.

"And you didn't *tell* me?" screeched Patsy. "Elaine, you secretive old thing! You're a granny! Congratulations!"

She leaned across and flung her arms round Elaine.

"Come on," she said as she felt her tense up. "Relax. OK, that's your line – but I'm your friend, remember?"

Is she? I hadn't realized.

Tears came into her eyes and she didn't try to stop them. She let her head drop onto Patsy's shoulder.

"You've been great," Patsy said. "You stood by Cal and you've been wonderfully kind to Kerry. And I don't know what you've done to Fergus, but he's very nearly cheerful these days."

She was rubbing the back of Elaine's neck gently.

"And let me tell you," she went on, "there's nobody in the world who could have done more for Andrew than you did. He's a cat that walks by himself, but you got closer to him than anyone ever has."

"Not close enough," said Elaine.

Nothing is ever close enough.

"Why are you so hard on yourself?" asked Patsy. "We're not perfect. We do the best we can. You've done a great job, Elaine. You'll go on doing a great job. That's enough. So stop beating yourself up. Just enjoy your life."

Elaine managed a shaky laugh.

"I've told so many people that," she said.

"Yeah, well," said Patsy, handing her a tissue. "That's what friends are for. Drink your tea."

The tide's up, so the ferry's riding high and the gangway slopes up steeply. It's quite windy and the mooring ropes are creaking against the bollards. Cars and trucks are starting to roll off onto the mainland. I'm standing with everyone else at the barrier, waiting for the guy to let us on and take the tickets.

Someone nudges me. It's Jess.

"Hi," she says. "How does it feel, being a dad?"

No-one's heard, but all the same...

"Shut up," I say. "What are you doing here? Aren't you in college? And how did you know, anyway?"

"Mum phoned. I didn't have a class this afternoon so I thought I'd do a flying visit. I'll go back tomorrow morning, no-one will miss me. That's a good thing about changing courses – they both assume I'm somewhere else."

We're all starting up the gangplank. At the top, Jess makes for the stairs that lead to the outside deck. "I'm fresh-air deprived," she says over her shoulder. "I never get outside these days."

Nobody else is daft enough to be up here, it's freezing. We sit on the red plastic seats by the side of the funnel and watch the gulls wheeling and screaming. At least the sun's shining.

"That's better," Jess says. "I get fed up with stuffy buildings."

First I've heard of it. She's never been the outdoor sort.

"How's it going at home?" she asks.

"OK."

"Pop's so funny, you know. Ever since I changed to music, he's taken to phoning me, asking how it's going. I asked if he was sure he didn't mind, and he said he was musical himself, so it was natural his children took after him."

"Must be joking," I say.

But he did start me off on the guitar, and he really wasn't bad. Maybe he wanted to do music himself. What if he got talked out of it by his own dad? I remember the old man, just about. Always wore a collar and tie, even if he was in a boiler suit. He set up the firm. McCasky likes such grotty old stuff, I never thought he had music in his head, but maybe he has.

Jess is fishing in her bag. She gets out a solid thing wrapped in newspaper.

"I brought you this," she says. "For the wee one."

It's a tortoise made of wood, with wheels instead of

feet. Where its shell should be there's a laminated wooden ball with dark and light stripes. I push it along the deck from my right hand to my left, and the stripy ball turns round as it goes along, so the pattern changes.

"Hey, cool," I say.

"Stupid, really, but I didn't know what to get."

"It's great."

We're both smiling.

"What's his name?" Jess asks.

"The tortoise?"

"No, idiot, the baby."

"Bardo."

"As in Brigitte Bardot? The film star?"

"As in Bardo McCasky." Saying the name is a thrill. "It means water."

"Nice," says Jess. "Is it Aboriginal?"

"Yes."

She nods. After a minute, she says, "I really am pleased, you know. I'm going to enjoy being an aunt. I won't be much help or anything, but if there's anything I can do… Can't think what, but you've only got to phone. Any time. From anywhere."

"Sure. Thanks."

That's why she came up here. We couldn't have talked in the cafeteria, with people all round. Might even have been Bill. Heaven forbid.

There's a rumbling roar and a billow of smoke from the

funnel as the engines start up, then a ding-dong from the tannoy for the captain's announcement. I pick the tortoise up in case it rolls across the deck as the boat moves away from the pier.

By the time the safety recording's over, we're out past the lighthouse and the wind is really cold.

Jess says, "That's enough fresh air. I'm going for a coffee. You want one?"

"Wouldn't mind."

She opens her bag for me to put the tortoise and its wrappings back in, then we head off across the deck. Jess hauls at the stiff-sprung door and steps over the ledge that keeps water out, and while she's doing that I look back. The broken path the boat has made curls away through the water behind us. Looking ahead, the lifeboats on their white-painted davits block the view.

I guess that's the way it is.

We head down to the warm interior and the smell of chips.

About the author

Alison Prince has written over forty books, including *The Sherwood Hero* (Winner of the Guardian Children's Fiction Prize); *Second Chance* (Winner of the Scottish Children's Book Award); *How's Business* (shortlisted for the Smarties Book Prize) and *The Summerhouse*. She is also a journalist and poet, and plays clarinet in a jazz band.

See www.alisonprince.co.uk